A Note to Readers

Three generations of Smiths have grown up in Boston since Phillip and Leah had their adventures in *Fire by Night*. Phillip became an apothecary as he had always dreamed. He married and had six children, one of whom was the grandfather of Beth and Will, the children you will meet in this book.

While the Smith family is fictional, characters in this book such as Colonel Nicholson, Judge Sewall, and Governor Dudley are real. They made important decisions that affected the lives of the Boston colonists during Queen Anne's War.

Judge Sewall wrote a diary that tells us a lot about life in Boston during this time. Boys and girls went to different schools, and boys usually left school and were apprenticed to a trade when they were about twelve years old. Judge Sewall's son actually started going to school when he was only two years and seven months old!

While the colonists fought Queen Anne's War in America, England was also fighting against France and Spain in Europe. This is why the queen did not send as many British troops to the colonies as they wanted.

QUEEN ANNE'S WAR

JoAnn A. Grote

BARBOUR
PUBLISHING, INC.
Uhrichsville, Ohio

Published by Barbour Publishing, Inc., P.O. Box 719, Uhrichsville, Ohio 44683
http://www.barbourbooks.com

ecpa Member of the
Evangelical Christian
Publishers Association

Printed in the United States of America.

Cover illustration by Peter Pagano.
Inside illustrations by Adam Wallenta.

CHAPTER ONE

Whose Ships?
Saturday, July 15, 1710

The schoolmaster rapped his cane against the rectangular wooden table at the front of the room. "Boys! I *will* have your attention!"

William Smith pulled his gaze from the second-story windows overlooking the Boston street with an effort and forced his attention to the instructor in the black, knee-length coat and breeches. The buzz of boys' voices around him stopped, but he noted a number of the youngsters' necks stretched above their linen shirts as the boys attempted to see what was causing such a stir in the street below.

Men's and women's voices came in North Writing School's second-story window, mixed with the sounds of trampling feet and horses' hooves, the rattle and thump of cart and carriage wheels—far more noisy than the normal sounds of vendors going about their daily trade.

"Eyes forward, young masters." The schoolmaster stood straight and still, glancing about the room, the long white curls of his fashionable wig resting on his shoulders. Boys' heads obediently but slowly swiveled toward the grim-faced man. "I expect there will be no further disruptions. I should hate to be compelled to apply the cane to any young hands on such a sunny day."

Will was certain that every boy in the room was bursting inside to know what was happening outside, just as he was, but none of them would speak back to Master Evans. They all knew he would not hesitate to make good his threat of punishment.

"Now," the schoolmaster continued, "if Master William will continue reciting the subtraction ciphering, perhaps he can complete a decent day's work before we break for the noon meal."

Will started to stand.

Boom!

The blast echoing over the nearby bay left the room in stunned silence.

"A cannon!" someone shouted.

Everyone in the classroom knew that a cannon blast was the signal that Castle Island, which guarded Boston's harbor, had spotted an unknown warship. Will's blood ran cold.

He rushed to the window and the rest of the boys followed. He stared at the bay, trying to see Castle Island and the flags it would raise to let the town know whether the ships were friendly or not. He couldn't, of course. It was too far away, almost two miles from Boston.

Had Nicholson convinced Queen Anne to send warships to

help the colonists fight the French? Would an entire fleet of English men-of-war and transports soon rest in the harbor?

"Maybe it's the French." His friend Jeremy's whisper sent shivers down Will's back.

The colonists had been fighting the French for control of the New England lands since before he and Jeremy were born. Lately rumors had filled the town that the French were planning to attack Boston. *And why wouldn't they want to capture it?* Will wondered. It was the largest town in the American colonies, with the most active port.

The French had attacked forty merchant vessels along the coast last year. *Pirates, they were,* Will thought with disgust, *capturing ships, taking sailors prisoner, and stealing the cargo.* Over a dozen ships had been attacked this spring, some almost within sight of Boston.

Will shoved a hand impatiently through his short blond hair and tried to brush off the fear Jeremy's whisper had started. "Maybe it's not the French. Maybe it's Colonel Nicholson returning from England with more marines."

Boom!

A second cannon blast set Will's heart beating faster than the waves against the Boston wharves during a bad storm.

Boys started racing for the door. Master Evans didn't even try to stop them. He just stared out the windows.

"Come on." Will poked Jeremy's arm. "Let's go to the town house. The town leaders there are sure to be the first to know what's happening."

He whirled from the window, raced across the room, and was soon out on the crowded, narrow lane. He was the fastest runner at North Writing School, but his ability did him no good today; one couldn't run in this mass of people. He guessed all of Boston's almost nine thousand people were heading toward the town house or harbor.

Jeremy Clark hurried along beside him. Jeremy was eleven, the same as Will, but he was short and stocky with dark hair that waved inches below his ears, where Will was tall and slender with blond hair that barely covered the collars of his linen shirt and a long vest in back. They'd been attending North Writing School together for years, and Will couldn't remember a time they hadn't known each other.

Drums began their rat-a-tat beat, calling the town militia to arms, while Will and Jeremy worked their way through the crowd. Men with muskets and grim faces pushed their way down the winding street, headed for the two fortlike batteries at each end of town that guarded Boston. If the ships belonged to the enemy, they would be there to repel the attack. If the ships were friendly, they would welcome the incoming troops.

Will and Jeremy dodged the elbows of merchants in their fancy jackets trimmed with gold and lace and the marketing baskets that hung on women's arms to gain a bit of ground. They hurried around a vendor whose one-wheeled cart was filled with fresh, colorful vegetables.

The wooden town house, which stood square in the middle of King Street, was surrounded by people. They crowded about the twenty-one ten-foot-high pillars that supported the two-story building where New England's laws were made.

It wasn't the laws or the governor or the colonies' leaders who filled Will's mind at the moment. All his attention, and that of the crowd, was focused on the top of the building. A railing enclosed the captain's walk, a fifteen-foot-wide area on top of the building where ships' captains went while in town to check on their ships.

A number of Boston's town leaders were on the walk, along with some ships' captains, all holding long telescopes aimed over the bay. Will recognized Judge Sewall, an older man dressed in his usual somber black coat, his long white hair waving over his shoulders.

The printer of New England's only newspaper, the *Boston News-Letter,* stood in front of Will and Jeremy, his ink-stained leather apron covering his shirt and leather knee breeches. He cupped his hands about his mouth, put back his head, and called, "Judge Sewall, what do you see?"

The judge leaned against the railing and looked down at the crowd. "A flag has been hoisted at the castle."

Will's heart slammed against his chest. A warship!

The crowd buzzed with concern. Jeremy grabbed his arm. Were his own eyes as big and dark with fear as Jeremy's?

The printer's head tipped back again. "French ships or English?"

"Too soon to tell!"

Boom!

The crowd went silent at the cannon blast.

Boom!

Will's stomach felt like he'd just drunk a mug of soured milk. Two cannon shots to confirm the flag. There were two men-of-war in the channel between the ocean and Castle William.

He nudged Jeremy. "We'd better get home. Our parents will be looking for us."

Jeremy's eyebrows shot up beneath his long brown hair. "But the men-of-war! We have to wait until we know whether they're friendly."

"The ships can't get to Boston without going past Castle Island. We'll know then whether they're friendly. If they aren't, the fort at the island will fire on the ships."

Jeremy's stocky shoulders drooped. "I suppose you're right, but I still think we should stay."

"Come on, let's go. Most likely the ships are with Colonel Nicholson."

As they started home, Will glanced down King Street to the bay. *What if the ships weren't friendly?* Fear slid down his backbone on droplets of sweat. *What if the town was about to be attacked?*

CHAPTER TWO
Men-of-War

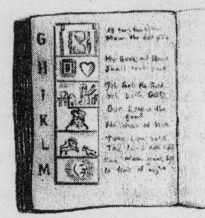

Will had never spent a more fidgety afternoon. All morning he'd studied the catechism, as all the boys did every Saturday at school. He'd memorized the piece for this week word for word. Now that it was time to recite it for the schoolmaster, he couldn't remember one sentence. His mind insisted on wandering to the bay, wondering how close the ships were. His ears were filled with the sound of the drums that never stopped.

Mr. Evans stood rigidly beside his table desk. "Master William, your catechism piece. Recite the question first, followed by the explanation."

"Uh, yes, sir." Will swallowed hard.

Footsteps drummed a hasty beat up the wooden stairs. A moment later the bookshop owner from the floor below burst into the room, his wig slipping from his head in his haste. "He's back, Mr. Evans! Nicholson is back from England!"

Will thought he could almost see relief washing through the room like a huge wave. Every face broke into a smile.

"Colonel Nicholson!"

"How many men-of-war did he bring?"

"Now we'll show those French!"

"Hurrah for Nicholson!"

The boys' eager cries and questions flew as they surged toward the shopkeeper. The rap of Evans's cane brought them to a sudden halt. "You've not been dismissed. Take your seats."

For a moment Will thought the students wouldn't obey, but they did, slowly. So did he, though he wanted nothing more than to run to the wharves.

"The old goat!" Jeremy whispered before slumping onto the bench beside him.

Will would never have dared put such a thought into words, but he felt just like Jeremy.

When everyone was seated, Mr. Evans turned solemnly to the shopkeeper. "Has Colonel Nicholson come ashore yet?"

"No."

"How many men-of-war did he bring?" Evans asked.

"Only the two the castle spotted earlier, the *Dragon* and the *Falmouth*."

"Two!" Will gripped the slanted desk in front of him. "But we were hoping for at least six, with a thousand marines. What can two ships do against the French?"

12

Mr. Evans's thin lips pressed together into a tight line. He glared at Will before he spoke. "Master William, you will not speak unless spoken to first."

"I beg pardon, Mr. Evans."

The shopkeeper shook his head. "I've no more news. I'd best be getting back to my shop."

He'd barely left the room before the last of the sand in the hourglass on Mr. Evans's desk dribbled through. "It's five o'clock, sir," Jeremy said, pointing to the glass.

Will bolted to his feet with the rest of the class. He'd thought the end of the school day would never come!

Mr. Evans gave him a thin smile. "It appears you've been spared your recitation for today. You shall give it first thing Monday morning. Perhaps you'll close this day for us in prayer."

"Yes, sir." Will bowed his head. "Thank Thee, Lord God, for Colonel Nicholson's safe return. Thank Thee for giving us the chance to go to school. Please keep us safe until we return here again. Amen."

"Dismissed."

The boys rushed for the door and raced down the narrow outside steps to the street. As if of one accord they headed toward the wharves.

Jeremy ran alongside Will. They were soon ahead of all the others.

"Will, wait for me!"

Will turned quickly to see his sister Beth dodging some of the younger boys in her attempt to reach him. The sun bounced off the golden curls waving behind her.

When she reached his side, she smiled up at him, her blue eyes shining with excitement. "Have you seen him yet? Have you seen the colonel?"

"Of course not. Likely he's not even off the *Dragon* yet."

"Is that the name of his warship?"

"It's called a man-of-war, and yes, that's the name."

"Do you think he's brought dozens of warships—I mean, men-of-war with him? And lots of soldiers?"

Will shrugged impatiently. "How should I know? So far, there are only two ships. And the soldiers he's brought are called marines."

"Oh." For two whole steps, she didn't say anything. Will was just about to say something to Jeremy when she spoke again. "You think Queen Anne wants to help us fight the French, though, don't you?"

"How would I know what the queen of England wants?"

"But—" Beth's comment was cut off when she fell to her knees.

Will grabbed one of her elbows and Jeremy grabbed the other, and they pulled her to her feet. They weren't quick enough to keep the boys behind them from bumping into her. "You'd think a nine-year-old girl could go through one entire day without tripping over her own feet," Will said, disgusted.

"I didn't fall over my own feet. I tripped over a stone."

"Well, watch where you're stepping." He reached for the square of linen in her hand. "It looks like you ruined whatever this is you stitched at dame school when you fell. It's dirty and torn."

She shrugged, lifting her pretty curls. "I don't care. It's only a handkerchief. I don't like sewing, anyway. I wish I could go to the kind of school you do."

Will shook his head. Beth never had liked to sew like other girls.

She sighed. "I wish Queen Anne would come from England with Colonel Nicholson."

Jeremy snorted.

14

Will laughed at her and shook his head. "Why would the queen want to come to the colonies?"

"To see them. If the colonies belonged to us, wouldn't you want to see them?"

"You have the most foolish ideas."

Beth adjusted the white cloth that tied over her shoulders. "You only think my ideas are foolish because you don't think of them first."

"Mmmm." He was tired of her chatter. It wasn't that he couldn't think of a good many things to speak on himself. He just preferred to mull them over in his own mind. When he did talk, he'd as soon speak of more important things than the shoemaker's dog chasing the cordwainer's chickens, or Mrs. Hitchcock's magnificent new gown from London—which were the types of things Beth usually talked about.

"One day," she continued, "I'm going to go to England and see the queen, no matter what you think."

Jeremy barked out a laugh and leaned in front of Will to say, "It's not likely the daughter of a cabinetmaker will be crossing the ocean to visit the queen of England."

Beth lifted her chin, her eyes sparking anger. "I will one day, Jeremy Clark. You'll see."

Jeremy grinned. "If you do, you'll probably fall flat on your face when you curtsy to her."

"You make me so mad!" She stamped her foot, but her small slipper made little sound, and Will couldn't keep back a smile. Beth always became angry when Jeremy teased her, which was why his friend badgered her each time they met.

The familiar smells of saltwater and dead fish enveloped them as they neared the waterfront. Will's heart started beating faster when they reached Scarlett's Wharf. Clerks with quill pens and wooden pads moved quickly about the wooden barrels of rum, molasses, coffee, and tea that stood large and heavy in front of the warehouses and counting houses lining the north side of the wharf. Sweaty dock workers rolled more barrels along the gray planks. Huge ropes lay in coils.

At the end of the wharf, Will looked out over the sail-filled bay. Excitement pounded in his chest. "Look!"

Out past the low-water mark, two men-of-war he hadn't seen before rode the waves. An English flag waved lazily from a mast on each ship.

Jeremy followed the direction of Will's pointing finger. "The warships."

Beth propped her fists on her hips. "They're called men-of-war."

Will gave her a disgusted look, but he noticed Jeremy, for once, ignored her.

"How many guns do you think they have, Will?"

"I don't know. Maybe the *Boston News-Letter* will tell us tomorrow."

Beth shook her head. "I don't know what you two are so excited about. They just look like a couple of large ships to me."

Sisters! Will thought, rolling his eyes at Jeremy.

"Think the marines will come ashore tonight?" Jeremy asked.

A dockhand passing by with a large trunk on his shoulder answered. "Naw. They can't come ashore until the town leaders say so. Officers will be here soon for a good meal at the Green Dragon Tavern, though, or I miss my guess."

Will swallowed his disappointment. He'd hoped to see some marines and maybe Colonel Nicholson.

Jeremy grinned. "Since we can't see any marines, maybe we should go swimming."

Will frowned at him. They often went swimming at dusk, off the less public piers, but not off a busy wharf. It wasn't allowed.

16

Jeremy was always pulling pranks, and pulling Will along with him.

"You know you can't go swimming," Beth said as they turned to leave.

Jeremy leaned close to whisper in Will's ear. "Slip out tonight and meet me for a swim."

Will nodded. The water would feel good after such a hot day. Besides, maybe they'd see Colonel Nicholson and some of his officers come ashore.

CHAPTER THREE

A Meeting with the Colonel

Will and Beth dropped Jeremy off at his father's combined home and cooper shop near the waterfront on Anne Street, named for Queen Anne. Through the open shop door, Will could see wooden barrels called hogsheads and wooden buckets all over the floor. Jeremy's father sat on his cooper's bench, shaving a barrel stave. Will waved at him, and Mr. Clark waved back. Mr. Clark made the best barrels in town, according to Will's dad.

Beth's chatter kept going nonstop. Will wondered how one person could talk so much and say so little. He supposed he should be used to it after all these years, but he wasn't. He usually let her talk on and on while his thoughts drifted in whatever direction they wished.

When Beth turned toward home, Will continued on to his father's cabinetmaker shop. He was glad his father's shop didn't adjoin his house, like Jeremy's father's shop. Mr. Smith had recently built a new home in North Boston. It wasn't as fancy as the homes of the wealthy merchants, but it was nice.

Will's sister Mary and her husband, Robert Allerton, lived above the shop now. Rob used to be an apprentice for Will's father. Now he was a journeyman—an experienced cabinet-maker—and worked in his father's shop.

A foot-high sign with a chest of drawers painted on it hung above the shop door to let people know what trade was practiced within. It squeaked as it swung in the hot breeze.

Cabinets, desks, beds, tables, and chairs in all stages of completion filled the largest of the shop's two rooms. The smaller room was used to store wood.

Will liked the smell of sawdust that always filled the shop. It was a pleasant fragrance that brought with it the scent of trees and outdoors. Some days the strong scent of glue or stinging odor of oils used to protect the furniture overpowered the sawdust, but not today.

Most of the days he wasn't in school Will spent in the shop doing errands and chores. Idleness and play weren't encouraged among either children or adults in Boston. Occasionally he was allowed to help oil and polish a finished piece or work on some simple item like a frame for a mirror, but more often he came no closer to working with the wood than turning the wheel Tim turned now.

Will loved working with wood. Sometimes his hands just itched to create fine furniture. He could tell what type of tree a piece of wood came from just from the smell: cedar, walnut, maple, cherry, pine, poplar, satinwood. One day he'd be a master cabinetmaker. His father had promised that he'd begin training him next year, when Will turned twelve, the same as if he were an apprentice.

Tim, the curly-haired, thirteen-year-old apprentice turning the huge wheel that ran the lathe, nodded a hello to him. Will glanced at Rob but didn't greet him. He was carving a spindle on the lathe, holding a long-handled, sharp gouge against the wood as the spindle turned. Will knew Rob couldn't afford to look away without chancing a mistake.

Dark-haired Charles, seventeen and also an apprentice, smiled at him and went back to cleaning up his workbench. Will knew his father expected all the tools to be put in their place at the end of each workday. Shelves along one wall were filled with planes, chisels, saws, gouges, clamps, and wooden patterns in many sizes. Drawers behind Charles were filled with pegs.

His father smiled at him from across the room, where he was wiping a rag over a maple chair. "Did you see the men-of-war in the harbor?"

"Yes, sir. Wish they could come right up to the wharves. Sure would be great to see one up close."

Rob pulled his long-handled gouge back from the spindle and straightened, and Tim let the wheel whir slowly to a stop.

"We went to the wharves, too," Rob said. "Only two warships arrived with Nicholson."

"With the ship already stationed here, that makes three," Charles said in his strong English accent. "I hope there are more on the way. We'll need them against the French forts."

"We're cabinetmakers, not war-makers," Mr. Smith reminded them quietly but firmly. "If Colonel Nicholson and Queen Anne have sought the Lord's guidance, surely their decisions regarding the military are wise and proper."

"Yes, sir." Charles and Rob murmured their agreement and

went back to work. But Will knew they wondered as he did about the many years the English and colonists had already been fighting the French with little success.

Didn't the Lord care that the French raided the English colonies' fishing and merchant ships? Only last year the French had captured over forty ships, some barely outside Boston's harbor. And what of the French organizing the Indians to join them in raiding farms and villages, killing people, burning their homes, and taking captives?

Will had started to slip his leather apron over his school clothes when his father said, "Will, I want you to run this over to the town house." He patted the top of the chair he'd just repaired. "The town leaders sent it to us to be repaired, since I made it for their assembly room years ago. The governor and the other leaders will likely be meeting with Colonel Nicholson this evening to find out what news the queen has sent them. They may need the chair."

"Yes, sir." Will picked up the heavy, high-backed chair.

"Mind you, don't tarry. Come directly home from the town house. And don't forget to bring the cow home from the common."

"Yes, sir."

Will hurried down Cornhill Street toward the town house, his heart pumping wildly beneath his shirt. He'd only been inside the meeting house a couple times. He never passed the building without a feeling of awe. The most important men in New England met there to make the most important decisions in New England.

He was breathing hard by the time he reached the third floor, where he knew the assembly room was located. He set the chair down and looked about him. He'd never been on this floor. Which way should he go?

A large hand rested on his shoulder. A deep voice said, "And where would you be going with that chair, lad?"

Will glanced up. An older man with a heavy white wig stood beside him. But it was the man's long red coat with its huge blue collar and sleeves that caught Will's attention.

Will's heart fell to his toes and bounced back up. "Colonel Nicholson!"

CHAPTER FOUR

Secret Plans

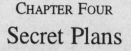

Colonel Nicholson smiled. "You know my name, but I don't know yours."

"Will." He gulped. "That is, William Smith, sir."

The colonel pointed at the chair. "And your chair, Master Smith?"

"It's for the assembly room, sir. I'm delivering it for my father. He repaired it."

"Ah, then your father would be Edward Smith, the cabinet-maker."

"Yes, sir." Imagine the colonel knowing of his father!

"He's one of the best in New England. I've seen examples of his work in some of Boston's finest homes."

Will grinned, proud that his father's work won the colonel's praise.

"The assembly room is at the other end of the floor." The large man bent slightly at the waist and said in a loud whisper, "I'd like to go up to the captain's walk and check on the harbor before I meet with Governor Dudley. Would you accompany me?"

Will gasped. "To the captain's walk? Truly? I've never been to the captain's walk!"

"Ah, then you must come. Every Boston boy should at least once have the pleasure of seeing the harbor from the town's best vantage point. But we must hurry. The governor and selectmen are awaiting me."

Nicholson led the way to the stairs in the middle of the building. Will forgot entirely about the chair and followed the colonel up into the open air of the captain's walk.

Will looked around him and gasped in delight. "I've never been able to see so far!"

Nicholson smiled. "If it weren't almost dark, you could see farther. Perhaps we can arrange it some day."

The colonel lifted his telescope and scanned the bay. Will leaned against the railing that surrounded the flat roof and tried to see everything.

After a minute or two, the colonel held his telescope toward Will. "See how much clearer things look through this. Careful, though. It's heavy."

Will held it as gingerly as though it were made of sugar. He couldn't believe he had the opportunity to look through such a wonderful invention, and the colonel's at that!

He held the small end against his eye, the brass ring cool against his skin. It took him a moment to steady the heavy instrument. The colonel showed him how to turn the sections in order to make the view clearer.

Will aimed the scope over the ships' masts, which filled the harbor like a forest of bare trees, and looked toward Castle William on Castle Island. "Why, I can see it as clearly as if I were standing beside it! I can see the flag of England flying from its post!"

He turned slowly, steadying the heavy instrument, and searched the harbor for the men-of-war. There! He'd spotted one! "I can see the *Dragon*. There's a cannon on the top deck! I can see it as plain as you please. And marines!"

"Do you wish to be a marine in the queen's navy one day, Will?"

"I think it would be exciting." Will lowered the scope and turned to the colonel. "Of course, I'll fight for England and the New England colonies when I'm a man. It would be wonderful to see other parts of the world. I've never been beyond Boston, except to Harvard on graduation day. And I've gone with Father to some estates on the other side of Charles River. Once we had to go almost five miles! But I'd like to see the West Indies, where the merchant ships bring molasses and sugar from. And Old England, where my great-great grandfather lived."

"It sounds like you'd make a fine marine."

"I wouldn't want to be a marine for life, sir. I want to be a cabinetmaker, like my father."

The colonel patted his shoulder. "The Lord calls each of us to His purpose."

"I'd like to go with you up north to fight the French," Will said eagerly. He lifted the scope and looked back at the *Dragon*. "And I'd like to ride on a man-of-war some day. I've never been on a ship so large. I've never been on anything larger than a sloop."

The colonel patiently guided Will's viewing, suggesting he look for this feature and that on the large ship. Will tried to see everything. He thought he could stay and look at things for the rest of life without growing tired.

But finally Colonel Nicholson said, "We must go inside now, lad. I've kept Governor Dudley waiting long enough. It is acceptable for a military man to check on his ships and men before entering the meeting, but even a colonel mustn't keep the governor waiting too long. Besides, it's growing dark. It will soon be candle-lighting time."

"Yes, sir." Will handed the telescope back, trying to ignore the reluctance that filled him at giving it up. He knew from the way townspeople talked that the governor wasn't a patient man. "Thank you for taking me up here. I'll never forget it."

When they reached the third floor, Will recognized the governor, Judge Sewall, and some of the other selectmen standing in the hall.

The governor frowned at Will, but before he could say anything, Colonel Nicholson said, "This fine lad's father repaired a chair for the assembly room. William just returned it."

The governor's face looked a little less stern. Will thought he and the other gentlemen looked hot in their wigs and the proper long jackets they wore over shirts and knee-length vests.

When Will brought the chair into the assembly room, one of the men was pouring apple cider into pewter mugs. It made Will realize he was thirsty. He'd have a mug of cider himself as soon as he got home.

He was almost to the door when Colonel Nicholson said, "Here, lad, have a mug of cider before you go. It's the least we can offer you for bringing the chair at such a late hour and on such a warm night."

Will took the mug gratefully, but he noticed the governor was scowling. *He must be anxious to hear what the queen had told Colonel Nicholson about the battles to be fought with the*

French, Will thought.

He stepped toward the door. "I'll drink this in the hall, sir."

He closed the door behind him, knowing the men would want their privacy. He took a long drink of the cool cider. It's tangy sweetness tasted wonderful. It smelled like apples in autumn.

"Dear Lord, we thank Thee for bringing Colonel Nicholson safely back from England."

Will started at the sound of the prayer. He hadn't realized he would be able to hear so well through the door. A minute later the prayer was over.

"Now, Colonel Nicholson, tell us what the queen had to say about our battles with the French." Will recognized the governor's voice.

He held his breath. He knew he should leave. Surely the great men in the next room did not intend anyone, let alone an eleven-year-old boy, to overhear their discussion. But everyone in the colonies wanted to know what the queen had said! Will just couldn't seem to make his feet move.

Nicholson answered in his deep voice. "Her Majesty, Queen Anne, has agreed to spare us what ships and men she can, but with England fighting the war elsewhere in the world, the numbers are less than we had hoped."

"How much less?" The governor didn't sound pleased.

"Five men-of-war. The *Dragon* and *Falmouth,* which I brought with me, the *Chester*, which has been stationed here in Boston Harbor, and two thirty-two-gun boats presently stationed in New York Harbor."

"We expected you to bring six ships!" the governor almost yelled.

"And none of the men-of-war mentioned have more than fifty guns." Will didn't recognize this speaker.

"What of the marines?" the governor asked. "Is the queen

27

sending a thousand, as we asked?"

"No, sir. We will have a total of four hundred British marines."

"Four hundred!"

"Yes, Governor. The colonies are to supply the rest of the men. Massachusetts Bay Colony is to raise nine hundred men to accompany us."

"Nine hundred! With the men already guarding the frontier, that will mean more than one-fifth of our men will be in service. It is impossible."

"It is what the queen demands."

"But we can't expect to defeat all the French forts in Canada with five small warships and thirteen hundred men."

"We aren't to attack on the grand scale we had hoped, Governor. We are only to attack the fort at Port Royal, in Nova Scotia."

No one said anything. Will was careful not to move. Were the men so upset they couldn't speak? No wonder. To attack only one fort when they'd hoped to overcome all the French soldiers and send them away from the new lands for good!

He heard someone clear his throat, and then Nicholson spoke again. "The town must provide food for the colonial men who serve, and for the British soldiers, also."

"Didn't the queen supply the British marines' needs?"

"Only for the sea trip, Governor."

"But Boston has a difficult enough time supplying her own needs. The townspeople aren't going to like this one bit."

Will set his empty mug quietly on the floor and tiptoed to the stairway. He'd best be leaving. Surely he'd heard the most important and interesting news. It wouldn't be wise to stay until one of the council found him eavesdropping.

It was dark when he reached the street. He hurried as quickly as he could toward the common to pick up their cow and then toward home. He had to be careful, as the moon wasn't yet out and there were no lights to guide him.

His thoughts raced. He couldn't wait until Monday, when he could tell his friends he'd actually met Colonel Nicholson!

CHAPTER FIVE
An Educated Turtle

Will wasn't disappointed with his schoolmates' reactions to his news. They crowded about him before class began Monday morning.

"What's the colonel like?"

"Did he tell you about any of the battles he's led?"

"Did he let you handle his sword?"

Will stuck his hands in the pockets of his knee-length vest, leaned one shoulder against the schoolroom wall, and answered their questions. He tried to act calm, but inside he felt like his stomach was leaping with excitement. When he told the others that the colonel let him use his telescope, the boys moaned in envy.

He wanted to tell them the news of the troops and men-of-war and the battle which would take place at Port Royal. He didn't dare. When he'd arrived home from the town house Saturday night, he'd told his father and Rob the news he'd overheard. His father had warned him sternly not to tell anyone else.

"It is easy for news to fall into the wrong hands in a port town like Boston," his father had said. "You wouldn't want the French to discover Nicholson's battle plans."

Of course not, Will thought. But it almost hurt to keep from telling his friends what he'd learned. Wouldn't they be impressed to find he knew where the marines and colonial soldiers would be fighting!

"Harump!"

At the schoolmaster's throat-clearing, the boys scurried to their seats. They stood quietly while Mr. Evans crossed to his desk. The cane he used because of his lame leg thumped softly against the wide wooden floorboards with every other step.

He surveyed them silently for a moment, then nodded and smiled slightly. "Good morning, lads."

"Good morning, Mr. Evans," the boys said together.

"Master Jeremy, please lead us in our morning prayers."

Will glanced out the corner of his eye at Jeremy, who was standing beside him. The edge of Jeremy's lip dug into his cheek for just a moment. Will knew Jeremy hated to be asked to lead prayers, but of course he would.

"Dear Lord," Jeremy began, "Please be with us today during

31

school hours. Help us to learn our lessons well. And help Will remember his catechism lesson from Saturday. Amen."

Will glared at Jeremy. Why did he have to remind Mr. Evans that Will hadn't recited his lesson before the classes were dismissed on Saturday?

Jeremy just grinned back at him, his brown eyes dancing with fun as always. Will didn't think it was funny.

All the boys in the room were chuckling at Jeremy's prayer.

"Master Jeremy!" schoolmaster Evans bellowed, rapping the tip of his cane against the floor.

The room quieted abruptly. Will could hear Jeremy beside him trying not to laugh.

"Master Jeremy," the schoolmaster repeated sternly, "there is no place for jest when speaking to the Lord. Our God deserves only our respect."

"Yes, sir. But Will might need help remembering his lesson."

Mr. Evans pinched his lips together and looked at the floor. Will strongly suspected he was trying not to laugh. The schoolmaster always punished students when they deserved it, but most of the time he was a kind man, for all his stern manner.

When he looked up, Will couldn't see any hint of amusement in his narrow face. "If your intent was to remind me that Will did not recite his lesson on Saturday, it was quite unnecessary. I had not forgotten."

"Yes, sir," Jeremy mumbled.

"You may recite the lesson for us now, Master William. The rest of you may be seated."

Will waited for the shuffle of the boys being seated to stop before he began. Boy, would he tell Jeremy a thing or two after school! He'd been hoping Mr. Evans would forget all about the catechism lesson. He knew it by heart two days ago. But with the men-of-war arriving and the excitement of meeting Colonel

Nicholson, he'd forgotten to practice it this morning.

He repeated it slowly, concentrating on one sentence at a time. He looked over Mr. Evans's shoulder at a knot in the wall to keep from being distracted by the other students. Twice he paused, not remembering the next sentence immediately. But he remembered them before Mr. Evans could reprimand him.

"Thank you, Master William. Not as well done as your normal recitations, but I will accept it under the circumstances."

Will breathed a sigh of relief and sat down.

"Now, Master Jeremy."

Jeremy's head jerked up in surprise.

"You may stand, Master Jeremy, and recite your catechism lesson."

The other boys chuckled. Jeremy's face grew red. He stood up and ran the palms of his hands down the sides of his breeches.

"Sir," Jeremy started, "I recited my piece Saturday."

"I am aware of that. You'll recite it again now."

Jeremy gulped and started his piece, stammering slightly. He did a rather poor job of it. Will was embarrassed for him, even though he had brought it on himself.

When he was done, Mr. Evans said, "Don't mind the mistakes too much, Master Jeremy."

Jeremy dropped to the hard bench with a grin.

Mr. Evans leaned on his cane and smiled slightly. "You can recite it again for us tomorrow, and each day thereafter until you recite it perfectly. I'm sure it won't hurt the rest of the boys to hear the words of wisdom a few extra times."

Jeremy's shoulders slumped. "Yes, sir."

"Master Jeremy," Evans continued, "do you recall the purpose of the colony's first education laws?"

"To make sure children could read so they could understand the Bible and the country's laws."

Evans smiled and nodded. "That is correct. It might be good for you to remember that the next time you're tempted to act up in class. School is meant to be a blessing to students, not a thorn."

"Yes, sir," he mumbled.

Almost an hour later the students were bent industriously over their writing assignment. The room was quiet except for the scratching of quill pens across parchment. Will concentrated on forming his letters evenly in straight lines, careful to keep any ink blots from dropping on the paper. Blots would require starting over.

The younger boys seated near the door snickered. Will held the tip of his quill over his inkwell and glanced at the boys. They were all staring at the leather bucket of drinking water that stood by the door.

Will could just barely hear the sound of splashing and scratching. What was causing the sounds?

The boys' muffled laughter caught Mr. Evans's attention. He frowned at the boys, but they didn't notice him. He stood and walked toward the door, his gray and brown eyebrows still drawn together.

"Oof!" Will grabbed his side where Jeremy had poked him with his elbow. Jeremy was grinning ear to ear.

Supporting himself with his cane, Mr. Evans leaned over and picked something out of the bucket. It was dark brown and green, and it moved. A turtle!

The entire class broke out in laughter.

The schoolmaster didn't laugh. He searched the room with his gaze. "Are any of you boys man enough to admit you put this poor creature in the drinking water?"

No one answered.

Boys covered their mouths with their hands to try to stop their laughter. It didn't work.

Jeremy winked at Will, and Will knew Jeremy was the one who'd brought the turtle to the classroom. Just like Jeremy. *He could be a good student,* Will thought, *if he spent half as much effort on his schoolwork as he did thinking up pranks.* Still, Will had to admire him this time. How had he managed to get the turtle into the bucket before school started without anyone seeing?

Mr. Evans stepped up to the boy nearest the water bucket. "Is this your work, Master James?"

The young boy stood up, his legs trembling. "No, sir. I didn't do it, honest."

Mr. Evans's gaze swept the room, finally resting on Jeremy.

Will glanced at his friend. Jeremy stared back at Mr. Evans with the most innocent expression Will had ever seen.

"Master Jeremy, perhaps you will be so good as to deliver this creature to a more suitable home."

"Yes, sir." Jeremy hurried forward to take the wiggling turtle.

Mr. Evans handed him the bucket. "We'll need fresh drinking water, too."

"Yes, sir." Jeremy took the bucket and dropped the turtle back into the water.

The class howled in laughter as Jeremy hurried out the door.

At the shop, Rob, Tim, and Charles laughed, too. Mr. Smith didn't laugh, but he smiled and shook his head.

Will changed to a dark calico shirt and leather breeches, put on his leather apron, and grabbed the straw broom. Before he could begin sweeping, his father said, "Why don't you work on the cover for the schoolmaster's candle box?"

Will went to work on it eagerly. The cover was a simple design. It was a thin, rectangular piece of wood. He screwed it to the workbench. Then he went to work, tapping at a chisel with a hammer, working his way around the rectangle in the middle of the piece to form a simple design.

Sweat broke out on his forehead as he worked. Beads of it dropped onto the wood and into the thin curls of wood shavings on his workbench. It was still hot out, even though his father had opened the door, the wooden shutters that covered the windows, and the windows themselves. The salty air from the bay mingled with the wood to form a pleasant scent.

Will was concentrating so hard on his work that he didn't notice Jeremy and his father enter the shop until he heard Jeremy's father speak.

"Hello, Edward. How is your business faring?"

Will's father smiled at Mr. Clark and brushed his hand against his leather apron. "As well as can be expected in these times. No businessman does as well as he would like with the war on."

"That's so," Mr. Clark agreed.

Will smiled at Jeremy, wondering what he and his father were doing here. He couldn't remember them ever visiting the shop together before.

Jeremy gave him a smile that quickly disappeared. He clutched his vest with one hand, then clasped his hands behind him, looking nervous.

"We've come on business, Edward," Mr. Clark began. He rested a large hand on Jeremy's shoulders. "My son will be twelve soon. He'll be ready to leave the writing school in a few months. He wants to be a cabinetmaker. I'd like to apprentice him to you."

"I see." Mr. Smith waved a hand toward the lathe where Tim and Charles were working. Behind them, Rob was staining a fine chest. "I'm afraid I don't need anymore help in my shop." He smiled kindly at Jeremy. "I'm sorry."

Jeremy bit his lips, looked at the floor, and nodded.

36

"Please reconsider, Edward," Mr. Clark said.

Will glanced at his father. Mr. Smith shook his head slightly. "I've simply no place for him. The cost of feeding and clothing an apprentice and training him for seven years. . ." He shrugged. "The cost is too high for help I don't need. There are other cabinetmakers in town. Perhaps one of them needs an apprentice."

"My son wishes to train under you. You're the best cabinetmaker in Massachusetts."

"I appreciate the compliment, but it doesn't change the facts."

Mr. Clark stepped up only inches from Mr. Smith and looked him right in the eye. "I want my son to learn from the best. Wouldn't you want the same for your own son?"

Will shifted his feet, the sawdust crunching softly beneath his shoes. Mr. Clark's face was red, and his angry voice made Will uncomfortable.

"As I've said, Mr. Clark, there are other cabinetmakers who may be glad to train your son."

"I'll be glad to pay you to take him on, though it would be hard on the rest of my family to do so."

Mr. Smith plopped his fists on his hips, looked at the sawdust-covered floor, and sighed. Finally he looked back at Mr. Clark. "Jeremy is a nice boy, but I've no time to waste training a young man who isn't willing to work hard."

"What makes you think Jeremy won't work as hard as anyone else?"

"He isn't diligent in his schoolwork."

"You can't compare school learning with work!"

"It is all I have to judge your son by. If he doesn't understand the importance of using time wisely in learning his lessons, what guarantee do I have that he will use my time well if I take him into my shop?"

"You have my word," Mr. Clark roared.

Mr. Smith shook his head slowly. "I'm sorry."

Tim, Charles, and Robert were all concentrating hard on their work, but Will knew they were as uncomfortable as he was at the scene before them. Tim kept the huge wheel on the lathe pumping. It sent out a soft whir that did little to hide the men's voices. Will wished Mr. Clark had waited to approach his father in private. He was embarrassed, and he knew Jeremy must be, too.

Jeremy's eyes shimmered suspiciously, like he might be about to cry. He clenched his fists at his side. "Thank you for talking to us, Mr. Smith." He turned and ran from the shop.

Mr. Clark glared at Will's father, turned on his heel, and stalked out the door. Will watched him walk down the street, his shoes scattering pebbles, his shoulders hunched in anger. When Will finally turned around, his father was watching him.

"I'm sorry I couldn't apprentice your friend."

"Jeremy isn't bad, Father." If his father had only agreed to apprentice Jeremy, his friend wouldn't be feeling so bad.

"Do you think I'm unkind for not taking on Jeremy?"

Will looked at the cover of the candle box in his hands. He didn't answer. Eleven-year-old boys had no place telling their fathers they were wrong.

His father came closer and rested his hands on Will's shoulders. "It's his father's duty to teach Jeremy to value his time. Time cannot be replaced. It mustn't be wasted. If Jeremy understood that, I would have found a way to apprentice him."

Will nodded. "Yes, sir."

His father sighed and went back to his work. Will rubbed his hand absently over the piece of wood in his hands. He wanted to go after Jeremy and talk to him, but he knew Jeremy wouldn't want to talk to anyone right now. Mostly, he wished he hadn't been there to see his friend's embarrassment. He didn't know what he'd say to Jeremy tomorrow at school.

CHAPTER SIX
Rob's Decision

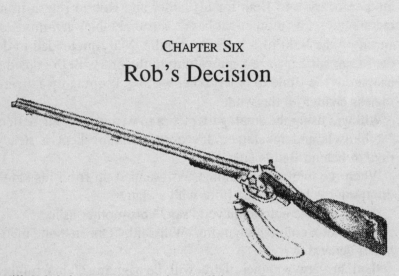

Will didn't have to worry about talking to Jeremy. Jeremy didn't mention what happened at the shop, so Will didn't mention it either.

Jeremy told more jokes than usual that day. Will knew he was just uncomfortable about what had happened and hoped Will would forget it. So Will grinned at all the right times and pretended he didn't know what Jeremy was doing. Still, it was the longest day of school Will could remember in a long time. For the first time, he wished Jeremy didn't sit next to him.

During the afternoon, all the students were restless. Colonel Nicholson had called a meeting for all the town's men that evening. Whenever Mr. Evans left them for a moment, the boys buzzed with questions. What would the colonel have to tell the men?

Will just smiled smugly. He already knew, but he didn't let on to the others.

That evening Will waited impatiently in the parlor with his mother, Mary, and Beth for his father and Rob to return from the meeting. His mother sat beside a round table, hemming an apron by the light of a bayberry candle. Mary pretended to do the same, but her gaze kept drifting to the entry. Beth copied a chapter of the Bible to practice her writing, keeping up a meaningless chatter all the while.

Will was using the small garter loom to weave stocking garters for himself and his father. It's quiet "thump" kept a steady rhythm behind Beth's talk.

When the men arrived home, Will leaped up from his stool, dropping the loom to the floor with a clatter.

"What did the colonel have to say?" his mother asked.

"He's not a colonel anymore," Will said. "Queen Anne made him a general."

"Did he say whether there will be fighting?" his mother asked.

"Yes," his father replied. "It's as Will said. Soldiers from the colonies will join forces with the English marines and attack the French on the St. Lawrence River."

His mother bent her head over her sewing so Will couldn't see her eyes. "I hate to think of friends and neighbors being sent into battle again."

His father moved behind the high, straight back of the chair his mother was sitting in and rested his large hands on her shoulders. "They must do what they believe is right."

Rob cleared his throat. "The general says he needs nine

hundred more volunteers from Massachusetts."

"Nine hundred!" Mary exclaimed. "But so many of Massachusetts Bay's fighting-age men are enlisted. Who will run the shops and trades if so many more go to war?"

"If we don't stop the French, our shops and trades won't be worth running," Rob said. "They stop the ships that carry our goods to market and steal the cargo. It's impossible to make a profit." He gulped, twisting the hat he held in his hands. "Mary, I've volunteered to fight."

Will grinned. His chest swelled with pride in Rob. His brother-in-law was going to be a soldier!

"No!" Mary whispered, shaking her head.

Will stared at her, shocked. Didn't she know a man had a responsibility to defend his property and his neighbor's when the queen asked?

Mary grabbed Rob's arm. "You can't go. We've only been married a year. I don't want you to go off to war."

Will planted his elbows on his knees and dropped his chin into his hands. *Women!* he thought. *Why do they always have to be so emotional? They never understand the things a man has to do.*

Rob took both her hands in his. "Mary, you know I've wanted to do this for years. Ever since my family was killed in the raid on Deerfield six years ago, I've wanted to join the colonial forces. I was too young to join then. And I was apprenticed to your father until right before we married, so I couldn't join the soldiers then, either. Now I'm free to join, and I must. If it weren't for the French who urged the Indians to raid Deerfield, my family would still be alive. Instead, all of them are dead: my parents, my brothers, my little sister. I have no family left. I wouldn't feel right if I didn't avenge their deaths by fighting against the French."

"You do have a family left," Mary said. "You have me and the baby that's coming." She rested one hand on her round stomach. Only a few more months, and she and Rob's first child would be born, Will remembered.

Rob took a deep breath. "If the French aren't driven out, our child may not have a good life. We've been fighting this war since 1702, and we've fought the French in other wars before that. The English colonies have lost thousands of men in the battles. I want our child to live in peace."

The room was quiet. No one said anything. *Even Mary can't argue against peace,* Will thought. But the silence made him uncomfortable.

"He gets paid, Mary," Will offered, hoping to cheer her up. "He gets a month's pay right away, and a jacket, and a musket."

Mary just stared at him with eyes wet from unshed tears.

"Did the general have any other news?" Mother asked.

Father nodded. "The town must see to supplying food to the colonial soldiers and the British marines."

"But the town has difficulty meeting the needs of its own citizens!" Mother exclaimed.

"We'll have to make do. It's been suggested we eat salted meat until the fleet leaves and leave the fresh meat for the soldiers."

Mother sighed. "I suppose it's the least we can do."

Will stood up. "I wish I could volunteer with Rob. I'd love to show those French a thing or two."

"Your time will come," Father assured quietly.

"Yes, and all too soon," Mother added.

Will shook his head. He didn't understand at all. Why was everyone so glum? They should be celebrating. Rob had done a fine and honorable thing in volunteering to fight.

Mother stood and set her sewing on top of the basket beside the chair. "It's time for bed, Will and Beth."

On the way out of the room, Will stopped in front of Robert.

"I'm proud of you, Rob. You'll make a fine soldier."

Rob smiled at him, but it was a small smile compared to the one he'd worn on the way home from the meeting.

CHAPTER SEVEN
On Board the *Dragon*
August 1710

Will dashed out of the school building with Jeremy at his side. Together they raced through the narrow, winding streets toward the harbor.

Colonial volunteers had been pouring into the city, almost sixteen hundred in all. Most were from Massachusetts, but the rest came from other New England colonies.

Will rather liked the hurry of war. The streets were filled with colonial soldiers and colorful British marines. They bustled about, gathering supplies and provisions, their wooden carts creaking beneath their loads. On the wharves, sailors were busy loading provisions into sloops to be carried to the ships and transports.

Even the town's craftsmen had been ordered to assist in preparing for the battle ahead. All the carpenters in town had been ordered to help prepare the fleet. Massachusetts Colony was to supply fourteen transports, boats which would carry soldiers and marines.

His father, Rob, and his father's apprentices were all working at one of the shipyards. They'd been working there for a month now, ever since the day after the town meeting. He knew his father was losing business while he was forced to help the marines, but his father didn't complain about it. Mr. Smith considered it his duty to the colony and the queen to help the ships get ready for battle, even though he wasn't excited about the war.

Will thought it was much more exciting to go to a shipyard than to go to the shop every day. It was so busy! Each day he stopped to see his father after school. *It gave him a wonderful excuse to go to the wharves,* he thought, grinning to himself.

"They're pulling a ship up!" Will called over his shoulder to Jeremy. "Let's watch."

They were careful to keep safely out of the way while the men worked on the winches that pulled the small ship out of the water and into the stocks. From there, the bottom could be checked for possible repairs, and if needed, a tarlike substance called black stuff could be reapplied. The men's arms glistened with sweat and their faces were bent into wrinkles as they tugged at the huge ropes. The men grunted, groaned, and gasped for breath. Water poured from the ship's hull.

Will bent his head back until his neck hurt, trying to see the top of the ship. "I never get used to how huge a ship looks when it's out of the water."

"I know," Jeremy said. "There's almost as much of the ship below the water as on top of it."

Will turned away from the ship in regret. "I'd better find my father."

Jeremy sighed. "I wish my father was working in the shipyard. He's been ordered to make lots of barrels to help hold provisions for the soldiers, but he makes them at his shop, the same as every day."

"You're helping him, aren't you?"

"Yes, but I don't like the work."

Will looked past Jeremy and out at the water. He didn't know what to say. It made him uncomfortable knowing Jeremy wanted to be a carpenter instead of a cooper.

Jeremy waved. "I'd better get to the shop."

Will watched him walk through the crowd of men working on the ships, weaving his way around piles of wood, huge coils of thick ropes, and barrels of pitch. He didn't like the angry look in Jeremy's eyes when Jeremy talked about his father's work.

Will dodged a couple of men carrying large oak boards for a new flat-bottomed boat and hurried about the yard until he located his father. He was surprised to find him talking to General Nicholson and the captain of one of the men-of-war.

His father noticed Will and smiled at him. He beckoned to Will and introduced him to Captain Martin.

Will bent slightly at the waist in the respectful bow he'd been taught as a very young boy. "I'm honored to meet you, Captain."

The captain smiled. "The general tells me your father is the best cabinetmaker in Boston. Do you agree?"

Will's cheeks grew hot. "Yes, sir."

He felt his father's hand on his shoulder. "I appreciate the general's faith in me, Captain. Son, the captain has asked me to repair a damaged cabinet in his quarters."

Will's jaw dropped. He snapped it shut. "On the *Dragon*?"

Father nodded. "Yes. We're going out to the ship now. I'll find out what I'll need to repair the damage, and tomorrow I'll go back."

Will opened his mouth to ask if he could go along. He stopped just in time. His father wouldn't be pleased with such behavior in front of important men like the captain and general.

General Nicholson caught his hands behind him and rocked back and forth slightly. "Have you ever been on a man-of-war, William?"

He shook his head. "No, sir."

"I thought as much." The general's eyes twinkled beneath his gray brows. "Mr. Smith, would you object to your son joining you aboard the *Dragon*? I'll be accompanying you and Captain Martin out to the ship. I would consider it an honor to show young William about the ship while the captain shows you the work he wishes you to do."

Will could barely breathe. Would his father say yes?

"It is kind of you to offer, General, but I cannot ask you to spend your valuable time entertaining a boy."

Will's hopes plummeted as fast and straight as a gull diving toward the waves.

The general smiled. "I assure you, I should enjoy introducing Will to the ship. I have few chances for such pleasant pastimes during these days of war."

Will thought his grin would split his face.

They took a small boat manned by British sailors out past the low-water line, where the *Dragon* was anchored. When they stood up to board the ship, the sloop rocked in the water beside the man-of-war. Will's heart was in his throat when he had to climb up the steps on the outside of the ship to the entry port in the middle of the lower deck.

"Don't be afraid," Will whispered to himself, grabbing the thin railing. "It's just a ladder, and if I fall, the water doesn't hurt." He didn't want the general to think he was a coward, so he stared at the steps above him and refused to look at the dark water below.

Once on board, the captain led them all to his quarters. They passed a number of large black cannons on the way, all with their faces pointed at the walls. Will knew that when they were in battle, square wooden ports would open in front of each cannon so they could be fired at the enemy.

He had to be careful not to trip over ropes and supplies as he followed the men. The ship looked large from the outside, but inside he discovered every inch was important to carry all the supplies and people. Black leather buckets hung along the walls. "Fire is a more dangerous enemy to a ship than the French," the general told him.

The captain's cabin on the second deck was completely different from the rest of the ship. It was large and lined with beautiful wood. There was a large desk in the room. But the most surprising thing to Will was the cannon. The captain explained that it was important to be able to fire at the enemy from any part of the ship, and even the captain's personal room on a man-of-war wasn't to waste space by not having a gun.

The captain and Will's father began talking about the repair work to be done, and the general led Will up to the ship's top deck.

Will was glad to be in the light and fresh air again. The second deck was very dark, even with lanterns lit, and smelled of many people living in close quarters.

"The *Dragon's* an old ship," the general told him. "It's been in service for about fifty years."

"Fifty years!"

The general grinned at Will's exclamation. "It's still capable of handling what the sea and the enemy bring against it."

"Yes, sir." Will stopped beside a small cannon and reached out to run his hand across the thick black metal. "How many cannons are on the *Dragon*?"

"Fifty. Men-of-war are rated according to the number of cannons they carry."

"I know, sir. A ship with one hundred or more guns would be a First Rate. The *Dragon* must be a Fourth Rate."

"Very good, lad! It is indeed a Fourth Rate."

Will's chest swelled in pride. "How many cannons do the other men-of-war in the fleet carry?"

The general pursed his lips and looked at the sky as if trying to recall. "The *Chester*, which has been stationed here at Boston, is a fifty-gun ship, as you likely already know. The *Falmouth* has fifty guns, the *Feversham* thirty-six, and the *Lowestoft* thirty-two. Of course, there's the bomb ketch."

"What is a bomb ketch?"

"A shorter ship that carries bombs called mortars. Mortars are especially effective when attacking a fort from water, instead of in a ship-to-ship battle. You can recognize the bomb ketch easily, for its stern is painted pink."

Will laughed at the thought of a pink-sterned ship going into battle.

The general nodded at some long bars lying on the deck beside the cannon. One end was cup-shaped with a flat bottom. The other end had something that looked like a scoop attached. "These poles are used to load the cannon with powder and shot.

One reason cannons need to be long is so they can extend far enough out from the ship so that they will not start the ship on fire when they are fired."

Will thought of the loud noise the cannons at Castle William made. When only one was fired, it could be clearly heard in Boston, above all the noise of the town. He couldn't imagine how loud it must be in the midst of battle, when a fleet with six men-of-war were all firing their cannons! Just the thought of it made his blood race. "It must be awfully exciting to be in battle."

The general didn't answer, and Will looked up at him in surprise. The officer's face was sober, his eyes serious. Will thought he looked almost sad.

"Battle is a necessary evil, lad. We must be well-equipped to fight, and we hope to always win. Most important, we hope our cause is always honorable and just. But even when the right side wins, battles are always sad." The general ran his large hand across the top of the cannon. "Too many men who have manned the *Dragon's* cannons have been killed in battle."

Will licked his lips and shifted uncomfortably. "Then why do you fight?" he asked timidly.

"The French capture the English colonies' merchant ships, and they capture and kill people from the English colonies in the towns bordered by wilderness. Every country has an obligation to protect its people."

General Nicholson didn't seem anymore excited about the battle to come than Will's parents. Will didn't understand why all these people thought it such an awful thing for a man to lose his life in battle. Isn't that what heroes did: die for the things they believed in?

CHAPTER EIGHT
Trouble at School

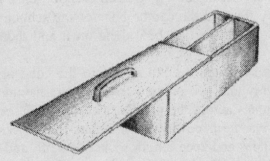

Will had a wonderful time telling his schoolmates about the ship the next day. They'd all seen the *Chester* in the harbor many times during the last few years, but not one of them had ever been aboard a man-of-war. They gathered about him before school, eager to hear what he'd seen.

Everyone except Jeremy, who leaned against the wall on the other side of the room and scowled.

"What's wrong?" Will asked as they slipped into their seats.

"Nothing." Jeremy slapped his catechism book onto the slanted desktop and didn't look at him.

Will shrugged. Maybe Jeremy would feel better later.

After eating at home that noon, Will hurried to meet his

51

schoolmates at Mill Pond for a few minutes of fun before going back to school. All the boys spent as much time as possible at the pond. There weren't many places in Boston that they could play in the water or fish or chase frogs or run races. Most places there were too many adults around reminding the boys not to waste time with such useless pursuits. But at the Mill Pond, they were beyond adults' eyes and ears.

Will liked the swampy smell by the pond and the sound of frogs and toads croaking and crickets chirping. It wasn't at all like Boston Harbor with its busy docks and wharves.

He carefully set the box he'd been carrying on a gray rock. He'd finally finished the candle box for the schoolmaster. He was proud of the fine job he'd done on it and didn't want it damaged.

He hurried through the tall weeds to the edge of the pond where Jeremy and two of their friends were having a contest skipping stones across the pond's smooth surface. A group of other boys was farther away. Their laughs and shrieks filled the air. Their shoes and knee-length socks were off, and they were stalking frogs among the reeds at the pond's edge.

Will picked up a flat, golden-colored stone. With an under-handed flick of his wrist, he sent it scooting over the water. *Three skips. Not bad,* he thought, smiling at Jeremy.

Jeremy didn't smile back. "I skipped my last throw five times."

"That's pretty good," Will said, leaning over to pick up another stone.

Jeremy skipped another stone. Will heard it "pop" twice as it touched the water.

Why was Jeremy so ornery lately? Will wondered. *Surely he wasn't still embarrassed that Will's father didn't apprentice him. It had been weeks since that happened.*

Joshua, standing on the other side of Jeremy, turned his

smiling, freckled face toward Will. "Tell us some more about the *Dragon*. You hardly got started this morning before Mr. Evans made us begin lessons."

Will tossed another stone, not even noticing how many times it skipped. It seemed lately his friends were always asking about the exciting things that were happening to him. He'd always gotten along well with everyone, but he was pretty quiet most of the time and not used to so much attention. He discovered he rather liked it.

"Did I tell you that the general said there's a new man-of-war that has something called a steering wheel? It's used to guide the rudder. The general says some day all large ships will have one."

Behind Joshua, Jeremy threw a stone toward the water. "As much time as you're spending with the officers, I'm surprised you haven't joined the marines."

Will stared at him, shocked. Jeremy's voice was angry. What had Will done to make him so mad?

Jeremy glared at him, his lips a thin, angry line. Then he turned and ran toward the boys who were chasing frogs. The younger boys' voices drifted down to Will and his friends, full of fun and laughter.

"Tell us about the captain's cabin," Joshua urged.

Will frowned after Jeremy, then turned and started describing the ship's largest, best furnished room.

When Will entered the schoolroom that afternoon, he set the candle box he'd worked on for so many hours on the schoolmaster's desk. The box's highly polished wood gleamed in the sunlight that poured through the high windows.

"Why, Master William, you've completed my candle box." Mr. Evans ran his fingers lightly over the smooth wood. "You've done beautiful work."

Will beamed. He felt proud and embarrassed at the same time. He'd never made anything for anyone outside his family before. No one else had ever complimented his work with wood.

He'd just taken his seat when the schoolmaster picked up the box. "Now perhaps the mice won't eat my candles at night," he said, smiling at the students. He slid back the top of the box. Something leaped out! It landed on his chest, right between his black jacket lapels, chin to chin with the schoolmaster.

Mr. Evans stared at the frog on his chest.

The frog stared right back.

"Croak!"

The students burst into laughter.

Mr. Evans screamed.

The frog leaped again, landing on Mr. Evans's head.

The schoolmaster hit at it. Missed.

The frog leaped again, knocking Mr. Evans's wig over his face. The frog landed on the desk, then took off again.

Mr. Evans slipped and sat down right on the floor. The curls of his wig peeked over the top of the desk at the students.

Will had never laughed so hard in his life. And he'd never seen such a large frog. One of the other boys must have put it in his box at the Mill Pond.

Beside him, Jeremy held his stomach and roared in laughter.

He gasped to catch his breath so he could speak. "I never thought you had the courage to pull a prank like that, Will."

"Me?"

"Master William!" Mr. Evans's voice was so thick with fury that it sounded like thunder.

Will's heart dropped to his stomach. He stopped laughing and stood up slowly. The other boys' laughter grew quieter, but Will noticed the snickers didn't stop.

Mr. Evans had pushed his wig out of his face and was struggling to stand. Will hurried to the desk and helped him to his feet, then handed him his cane.

Mr. Evans grabbed the cane and leaned on it, breathing heavily. "I would never have suspected you of such childish behavior."

Will gulped. "I'm sorry, sir. I didn't know about the frog."

"Croak!" The frog let out a loud complaint from the middle of the room.

"Get that thing out of here!" the teacher roared.

Three boys jumped up and dashed for the frog. It leaped at just the right time. The boys reached for it, missed, and fell in a pile.

The other boys laughed harder again.

Mr. Evans glared at Will.

More boys joined the chase.

The frog was faster.

Why couldn't the frog have been that good at getting away at Mill Pond? Will wondered.

"Catch it," Mr. Evans said to Will through clenched teeth.

"Yes, sir." Will hurried around the desk to join the others.

After many unsuccessful attempts, Will finally grabbed the frightened creature. It was so big that Will's hands barely fit around it. Will could feel its heart beating, and he knew the frog was frightened.

He hurried down the stairs to let the frog free outside. He could hear the boys' laughter all the way. He set the frog down in the tall grass at the back of the building and groaned. "Troublemaker," he accused the ugly creature. In all the years he'd been attending school, the class had never been this disrupted. Mr. Evans had never been angry at him before.

When he returned to the classroom, Mr. Evans was standing at the front of the class, waiting for him. Most of the students had stopped laughing, though Will noticed some of the boys were biting their lips to keep quiet.

"Master William, I'm very disappointed in you. I'd take the switch to your hands, but I'm too angry. I'm afraid I'd be overly severe."

Will gulped. "I didn't know about the frog, sir."

"Who do you think put it in your box if you didn't?"

"I. . .I don't know."

From a small shelf, Mr. Evans took a square of paper with a piece of rope attached. He handed it to Will. "You shall stand in front of the room for the rest of the day wearing this."

Will looked down at the paper in his hands. A large black L was drawn on it. He felt the blood drain from his face. L stood for liar. "But, sir, I am no liar."

Mr. Evans didn't even blink. "Put it on. You may stand beside my desk, facing the students."

Will swallowed hard. With shaking hands, he slipped the rope over his head. Then he turned to face the class.

While the students recited their lessons, Will studied their faces. Which one had done this? Was someone angry at him?

No. Most likely one of the boys just thought it would be a good joke.

He glanced at Jeremy and saw his friend was watching him. Jeremy glanced away quickly.

Could it have been Jeremy? Will wondered. *That was a stupid thought.* Jeremy was his best friend. It was just the kind of prank Jeremy would pull, but Jeremy would never let his friend take the punishment for it.

So who had done it?

CHAPTER NINE
Preparing for War

Will took a deep breath of the crisp September air. No school, no work, and it wasn't even Sunday! It was going to be a wonderful day.

He looked around the common and grinned. He could barely see the long grass for all the people. The entire town must have come out to see the British marines parade and the colonial soldiers muster. Tradesmen and their apprentices, merchants and clerks, selectmen and judges, sailors and docksmen, schoolmasters and students, young children and housewives were all here. Very little work would be done in Boston today!

Laughter and excited voices filled the common where usually only the quiet "moo" of pasturing cows and bird songs broke the silence.

The roll of drums sounded, and people hurried to the edge of the common. British marines fell into formal lines, standing at stiff attention behind the British drummers.

Will and Jeremy dropped down cross-legged in the long, cool grass and stared. "Look at them, Jeremy! Have you ever seen such a sight?"

"They're something to see, all right."

The marines in their bright red coats with huge blue cuffs and lapels, their black hats sitting on their heads like half-moons, and their muskets in hand were indeed a sight to behold.

"We've been looking all over for you!"

Will glanced up at Beth and their sister, Mary, standing beside him. Mary sat down gracefully, the way she did everything, and smoothed her skirt over her legs. Long lace from her short sleeves draped daintily over her elbow-length gloves. The sides of her blond hair were tied back in a green ribbon that matched her over-skirt, and her curls tumbled prettily over her shoulders. Will was almost as proud of lovely, ladylike Mary as he was of Rob.

Beth started to lower herself between him and Mary. She teetered, holding her arms out at her sides to balance herself, her skirt swaying over its wide hoop.

Will chuckled. Beth was obviously trying to imitate Mary and failing completely.

"Oof!" Beth grunted, plopping the last few inches onto the grass.

Jeremy chuckled. "Well, if it isn't Lady Beth."

He'd been calling her that ever since the day Nicholson had

landed with the warships, Will remembered.

"I will be a lady one day, Jeremy Clark." Beth tucked her legs to the side and smoothed her brown skirt over them, as Mary had done. Then she tried to smooth the red and white underskirt that formed a bright panel down the front of her dress. Will noticed there were already grass stains and dirt on it, though the day had hardly begun.

"You'll be sorry when I'm a lady, for I shan't buy anything from your shop, and I won't let my wealthy husband buy anything from you, either."

"You don't even know what kind of shop I'll have when I'm a man," Jeremy shot back. But Will noticed Jeremy was eyeing him warily. Did he think Will had told Beth their father wouldn't apprentice Jeremy? He hadn't.

"It doesn't matter." Beth brushed away a curl the wind had chased against her cheek. "We won't buy from any shop you own."

"At least she thinks I'll own my shop and not just be a journeyman," Jeremy muttered to Will.

Will grinned at him, relieved that Jeremy didn't seem to think he'd snitched to Beth. "Since when do you care what any girl thinks about you?"

"I don't!" Jeremy jerked his back straight.

The drums stopped, and the boys turned their attention to the brightly dressed troops. Colonel Twizleton called an order, and the marines swung as a group to the right.

Order after order was issued. The marines responded perfectly. Will thought they could have been one person, for they did everything in unison. The drums beat a different cadence for each order, and the marines moved in time with the beats. Will had never seen anything so spectacular. He'd watched the colonial troops muster before, but they weren't as well trained and disciplined as these British marines.

"I wish we had a tent," Beth yelled into his ear.

Will glanced at the row of tents lining one side of the common. The tent walls facing the common had been rolled up so the wealthy Bostonians inside on their chairs could view the events.

"We spend every day inside," he said. "I like it here where we can feel the sun and wind."

"Ladies don't like to sit in the grass. It dirties their gowns, and bugs crawl on them." She brushed an ant from her shoe.

Will snorted. Clumsy Beth was always getting her dresses dirty, and not because she sat on the ground.

Will suspected over an hour passed before the marines completed their grand display. Finally, it was time for the colonial soldiers to drill.

The colonials' brown and blue outfits weren't as spectacular as the British marines', and the troops weren't as well trained. When orders were called, many of the men stumbled about, watching those about them to see what they were to do. But Will could tell the crowd couldn't be prouder of the new soldiers.

"I heard there's about sixteen hundred colonial soldiers here," Jeremy said.

Will nodded. "Rob said one hundred Indians volunteered. Some of them are officers. Not all the tribes are our enemies."

Will's chest swelled in pride when he saw Rob among the other colonials. He pointed him out to Mary, who'd been eagerly scanning the soldiers for a glimpse of him.

"Look how good he is, Mary. He has the maneuvers memorized perfectly. He performs each one as soon as the order is given, without glancing at anyone to see what he should do."

"He does look especially fine, doesn't he?" Mary's hands were clasped tightly in her lap. She leaned forward slightly, her gaze glued on Rob in the midst of the men.

"He's the best of the lot." Will was glad to see her smiling. It was about time she acted proud that her husband was a soldier, defending the lands and rights of the colony and England.

He turned his attention back to the soldiers. A twinge of jealousy caught in his chest. He wished he were old enough to join them!

A couple hours later, Colonel Twizleton was finally satisfied with the colonials' maneuvers. One end of the common was cleared of people so the soldiers could practice their marksmanship. Will and Jeremy eagerly pushed their way to the best spot from which to see the men shoot.

The noise and smoke of the fired muskets sent a thrill along Will's nerves. He imagined himself holding the wooden butt against his shoulder, taking careful aim, and firing. He wished he could try it with Rob's new musket!

"Why do they have to be so loud?" Beth clapped her hands over her ears, disturbing her curls.

Will's gaze met Jeremy's over Beth's head. Jeremy rolled his eyes. "Girls!"

British marines called out good-natured jeers to the colonials. Will noticed some of them taking bets with sailors against the chances of the soldiers hitting their marks.

Will cheered wildly when it was Rob's turn to shoot. Jeremy and Beth joined in. Even Mary called encouragement to her husband.

Rob took aim and fired his first shot. The musket's kick jerked back his arm, and a small cloud of smoke rose in front of his face. His shot only nicked the target's edge.

"Why didn't he hit it?" Beth asked, hands still over her ears.

Will glanced at her in disgust and didn't answer. Disappointment dampened his spirits. It was almost as if Rob were performing for all the Smith family, and Will wanted Boston to know how well the town was represented by him. He watched impatiently while Rob refilled his musket, pouring in powder from the horn that hung around his neck, then placing a small lead ball in the chamber.

Will took a deep breath and cheered again.

Rob's next shots hit the mark, a couple almost at its center. Will smiled at Jeremy. Rob had proven himself to Boston.

When Jeremy and Will tired of watching the colonials shoot, they headed to the foot races in another part of the common. Beth tagged along, as always. Wherever they went, the sounds of musket fire and drums were in the background.

Will was itching to do something himself instead of just watching others. He reached for the slingshot in his back pocket. He'd carved the wooden handle for it himself from a piece of wood he'd found at his father's shop. "Challenge you to a match," he said to Jeremy.

"You're on."

At the back of the crowd, they located a tree with a low branch and chose a twig on it for a mark. It wasn't long before a crowd of boys gathered around them. Soon they had their own tournament going.

Neither Will nor Jeremy was the best of the group, but they didn't mind. It was fun just to be competing, challenging themselves the way the men were doing.

"How about a foot race?" Jeremy suggested when the slingshot match was over. The idea went over big with the others.

"Can I race, too?" Beth asked eagerly.

Jeremy snorted. "Of course not. Girls don't race."

"Why not?"

"Because they're girls."

"That's stupid. Will, I want to race."

"You can watch."

"Watching boys is boring."

"Why don't you stand at the end of the race and tell us who wins? That's important in case the race is close. You can yell for the beginning of the race, too."

"I'd rather race," she grumbled, but walked across the pasture toward the rock the boys had agreed would mark the end of the course.

Will lined up with the other boys and leaned forward slightly. His heart pumped faster just at the thought of the race. He kept his gaze on Beth where she stood beside the large gray rock.

She held up an arm. "Ready? Go!" The arm dropped.

Will darted forward. He loved to run, loved the feel of the wind against his face and through his hair, loved the power he felt as his legs carried him across the earth. He imagined his feet beating out a rhythm, like the drums beat out for the troops earlier.

He usually won the races. For just that reason, he knew the rest of the boys were out to beat him. Jeremy was his only real threat.

Jeremy was on his left. He'd started slower than Will, but Will saw out of the corner of his eye that they were about even now. Will tried to force his legs into a faster beat. His lungs hurt from the effort he demanded of them.

He could hear Jeremy's feet pounding the earth beside his own, hear Jeremy's heavy breathing. Would Jeremy finally beat him?

He stared at the rock and Beth. Almost there!

He flashed past the rock, Jeremy just a breath behind. The other boys followed quickly. He slowed to a jog and then stopped, panting.

Beth jumped up and down, clapping her hands. "You won, Will! You won!"

The rest of the boys slapped him on the back, congratulating him. Will was surprised to hear others calling out cheers for him, too. Looking around, he saw townspeople and soldiers had stopped to watch the race. Pride and embarrassment mixed together inside him at their attention.

"Good race, Will!" Rob called from a few feet away.

"Good shooting, Rob!" he called back, a warm feeling of comradeship in his chest.

Jeremy stood near, hands on his hips, breathing hard.

Will grinned at him. "Thought you had me there for a minute."

Jeremy didn't grin back. "Next time I will."

Is he angry because I won? Will wondered. He'd been friendly enough before the race. "I wouldn't be surprised," is all he said.

"You're a fleet-footed young man, Will. Congratulations."

Will glanced up in surprise at General Nicholson. His face grew hot. The general had watched him race! "Thank you, sir."

The boys parted to let the great man through, staring at him wide-eyed.

Beth grabbed Will's sleeve, jerked it, and whispered, "Is this General Nicholson?"

Will frowned at her and shrugged off her hand. "Yes."

"Who is this charming young woman?" the general asked.

"My sister Beth."

The general removed his wide black hat and bent low from his waist. "A pleasure to meet you."

Beth's face turned red, and for once, she didn't say anything.

"Is your entire family here?" the general asked Will.

"Yes, sir. We came to watch my brother-in-law." He pointed at Rob. "That's him. Would you like to meet him?"

"I'd be honored to meet a man who will be joining me in the fight."

Will tried to keep his face from showing the pride he felt when he led the general over to Rob and introduced them.

"I saw you shoot," the general said to Rob. "You are a good marksman."

Rob looked down at the musket in his hands. "I only hope my aim will be as good in battle, sir."

Will reached for the new musket. He held it up to his shoulder, pretending to sight along its barrel, and was surprised at how heavy it was. Rob had been given the queen's musket for volunteering, like the other men. Will wondered whether he would ever carry such a musket into battle.

The general was saying to Rob, "Your family has represented itself well today. You as a marksman and Will as a footman."

"I almost didn't win," Will admitted. "My best friend came within a hair of beating me. Did you see him?"

"Yes. He forced you to do your best, didn't he?"

Will nodded. He'd like to introduce Jeremy to the general. He looked around the crowd for him but couldn't see him. "Do you see Jeremy?" he asked Rob and Beth.

They both scanned the crowd, then shook their heads.

"Maybe you can meet him another time," he said to the general.

But he was disappointed. Where had Jeremy gone? Why would he have left when the general was there? All the rest of their friends had stayed. They were still standing around, whispering together and watching General Nicholson.

An uneasy feeling tightened his stomach. Jeremy hadn't been acting normal lately. He sure hoped nothing was wrong.

CHAPTER TEN

The Race
September 17, 1710

Where is everyone? Will wondered, walking down the aisle in the old church toward the front seats, where all the boys his age sat. The women and children filled their areas of the church, but the side with the men was half-empty.

He sat down beside Jeremy on the hard wooden pew. "Where are all the men?" he asked in a low voice.

"Helping get the fleet ready to sail. The ship captains asked all the craftsmen to work today. Isn't your father helping?"

Will stared at him. He could hardly believe his ears. "Working on Sunday? Of course not!"

Will was well aware that there were some tradesmen who often worked Sundays, but most were careful to go to church all day instead. His entire family and the apprentices were here today, like always.

The reverend was more upset than Will that so many were working. His displeasure was plain on his narrow face with its long nose. "Remember the Lord's Day to keep it holy."

Will jumped at the Reverend Increase Mather's loud voice repeating the third commandment. Will adjusted his shoulder blades against the back of the pew and gave all his attention to the pastor. His father would quiz him, Beth, and the apprentices later on what the pastor said.

"The Lord only asked us to set aside one day each week to spend time with Him." The Reverend Mather shook his head, the curls of his wig brushing the shoulders of his black frock. "How it must sadden Him to see Boston eagerly rushing about preparing for battle instead of praying. We must remember that our safety in war depends not only on good weapons, but even more upon God's grace."

Will tried to pay attention to the sermon, but his mind did wander as the hours passed. When the deacon turned the large hourglass that was used to keep track of passing time, Will watched the sand running through the narrow midpoint in a fine stream and wished it would run faster.

He was glad when noon finally arrived. His stomach had been growling since the last turn of the hourglass, even though there was only a cold meal to look forward to. Housewives didn't work on Sundays, either, though Will sometimes wished they did so he could have a hot meal.

When the family returned for the afternoon service, Jeremy

met him in front of the church. The rest of his family went inside, but Jeremy pulled Will aside.

One look at Jeremy and Will knew he was planning something he shouldn't do. His face was red, and his brown eyes were bright with excitement. "I don't know what you've got in mind," Will said, "but count me out."

Jeremy's grin widened. "There's going to be a horse race between some colonial soldiers and British marines. James is going to race."

"How did your brother get involved?"

"He and some other colonial soldiers got into an argument with some British marines last night at one of the taverns. The marines said the colonials couldn't even sit a horse, so James challenged them to a race."

Just like James, Will thought. He liked excitement as much as Jeremy. Will wasn't surprised he'd been out late with the others. With the soldiers and marines in town, he'd often heard men laughing in the streets long after the nine o'clock curfew. "When will the race be?"

"This afternoon. It starts on the common, then down to Cornhill, and back to the common by way of Queen Street."

"That will take them right past the church. It will disrupt services. Besides, it's against the town law to race on Sundays. What if the constable catches them?"

Jeremy shrugged. "That's not my worry. I'm going to go watch. Are you coming?"

"Church is almost ready to start." Will couldn't remember ever missing church, except when he was sick. "What will your father say?"

"Father is working. He won't know I'm not in church. And mother is too busy keeping my two little brothers and sister quiet to notice whether I'm with the rest of the boys down front in church. Come with me."

"My father is in church, and he will notice if I'm missing."

"Chickenheart! Just come see the horses, then."

Will glanced about. The street was filled with people on their way to services. Maybe he did have time to go see the horses. It was certainly tempting. He took a deep breath and bit his lips. Should he go?

Church bells began ringing. Will sighed. "There isn't time."

"Don't be a chickenheart. Stay and see the fun."

"I can't."

Jeremy shot him a look of disgust and walked away.

Will bit his bottom lip. He hated to be branded a coward. Sometimes it seemed a boy just had to disobey, like when the weather was furiously hot and the harbor just begged you to jump in and cool off. But he'd never been close to something that was out-and-out illegal before, like horse racing on Sunday.

He turned toward the church and noticed the deacon and constable making their way toward the common. They must have heard the rumors about the race.

Seated in his usual place a few minutes later, he heard hooves beat a loud staccato against the paved street in Boston's Sunday quiet. Will glanced at the windows. The deacon and constable must not have reached the common in time to stop the race after all!

A boy a couple years younger than himself darted to a window. A moment later he was followed by another and another. Will grasped the edge of his pew to keep from joining them.

Six men jumped up and hurried to the windows to shoo the boys back to their seats. Will wondered whether they went only to reprimand the boys, or partly because they wanted to see the race themselves.

How he would love to see that race! Would James win?

69

Imagine sitting atop a horse's powerful muscles, moving through space at such incredible speed!

The sound of hooves and cheering men faded. Suddenly Will was aware that the entire church was still. He glanced around. Disapproval and shock sat on every face—except those belonging to the boys in the congregation. Most of their faces showed excitement and a longing to see what was happening.

But as much as Will would have liked to see that race, he knew the men should have waited for another time. It wasn't proper to interrupt people's worship.

The church door slammed. Will swung around to see what was happening, and his jaw dropped.

The deacon held his father's apprentice Tim and Jeremy by the collars of their knee-length coats. He marched them down the aisle to seats at the very front while the entire church watched. Tim's face was red all the way to the roots of his curly brown hair. Jeremy's eyes flashed with anger at being caught.

Will hadn't even noticed until then that Tim had skipped church. He felt sorry for both boys, being embarrassed in front of everyone like that. But part of him was relieved. *If I'd gone with Jeremy, it might have been me being paraded down the aisle.*

The Reverend Increase Mather went back to his interrupted sermon. Then he led the congregation in prayer for the soldiers and marines who would be leaving Boston in a couple days for battle, asking God to give the officers wisdom and keep the men safe. Will knew he was even praying for the men who were working instead of attending church and for those who had raced.

Tomorrow the fleet would leave for Port Royal. All the churches would be filled with prayers for the battle. Surely with so many people praying, the Lord would see that the English won the battle. Wouldn't He?

CHAPTER ELEVEN
In Trouble

Will's usually patient father frowned down at Tim when they met after the service on Queen Street between the church and the town house, but he only said, "We'll speak of this at home."

Beth wasn't so thoughtful. As Mother and Father walked on ahead, her blue eyes snapped in excitement and she bounced up and down beside Tim. "You're in trouble now, Timothy Cutter!"

He scowled at her. Will knew he wanted her to be quiet, but didn't dare say so. He was in enough trouble already.

"Father's face turned almost purple when he saw the deacon

dragging you down the aisle by your collar."

"He wasn't dragging me," Tim muttered between clenched teeth. "I walked."

"It didn't look like it to me."

He glared at her and walked faster.

Will grabbed her arm. "Leave him alone, Beth." Weren't things bad enough for Tim without a pesty girl to rub salt in a man's wounds?

Beth stopped abruptly. She looked up at him with eyes that had the same innocent look in them that the cat's had when she'd tipped over the bucket of milk after he milked the cow yesterday.

"But he's the one who skipped church."

"Maybe it wasn't all his fault." Jeremy's older brother, James, was as bad at dragging Tim into trouble as Jeremy was at trying to drag Will into trouble, though Tim was two years younger than James. Will could remember a number of times his father's youngest apprentice had been caught and reprimanded after some prank James talked him into joining.

Shame squirmed inside Will's chest. The real reason he was defending Tim was that he'd almost been guilty of the same thing himself.

As they approached the fine new brick house they'd moved into only months earlier, Will frowned. "Father, what's that British marine doing outside our home?"

"I don't know."

Will studied the marine, who held the reins of a horse attached to a cart in the middle of the street. The bed of the cart was piled high with barrels, buckets, and baskets of food and blankets.

Just as the Smiths reached their door, a British officer and a colonial officer came out of their next-door neighbor's. The colonial officer raised an arm and haled, "Mr. Smith!"

Mr. Smith, Will, and Tim waited by their door for the men

to join them while Mrs. Smith and Beth went inside. Surprise pushed away Will's thoughts of the horse race and Tim's possible punishment. What could the officers be doing here on the Lord's Day?

"How may I be of service to you, officers?" Mr. Smith's voice was polite, but his thin eyebrows drew together in puzzlement.

The colonial officer bowed slightly. "Mr. Smith, it's been determined more provisions are necessary to supply the troops with food during the voyage. We've been ordered to search all homes and take whatever the troops can use."

Will gasped. The British officer darted him a quick look from steely blue eyes.

Mr. Smith stared at the officers as if stunned.

The colonial officer cleared his throat. "Please accept our apology for entering your home on such a mission on the Lord's Day, Mr. Smith, but the troops need provisions."

Mr. Smith nodded briskly. "Of course they do. They are welcome to all we can spare."

He ushered them through the dining room and toward the kitchen.

Will turned to Tim. "How did you get out of church today without Father noticing?"

"Told your father I had to use the necessary." Tim stuck his hands into his breeches pockets and swaggered a bit. "Once I was outside, I just kept going."

It sounded so simple. *Such a thing would never have occurred to me,* Will thought. *Guess I just don't like feeling guilty.*

"It was a great race." Tim's eyes shone with the memory. "Even if I do have to pay the price for watching it. James Clark won."

Will grinned. "I'm glad the colonials made a good showing, anyway."

Beth darted into the entryway. "Father says you're to help the officers carry provisions outside." Her breathlessness showed her excitement.

In the shed behind the kitchen, the officers asked what was in barrels, looked inside whatever they pleased, and ordered the boys to carry things out without even asking Mr. Smith's permission.

Tim and Will made several trips from the shed, carrying heavy wooden hogsheads of wheat flour, corn flour, and apple cider, and armloads of pumpkins and squash to the street, where a cart was waiting, attended by a British marine. Will determinedly ignored the anguished look in his mother's eyes as they passed her. He knew she was wondering how they were going to be able to replace all that food before winter set in.

The British officer indicated Will was to take some salted pork out next. Will was reaching for it when his father said quietly, "My family has been eating salted meat in order to spare fresh meat for the troops. My wife has given up a number of our chickens for the men, also."

The officers exchanged glances, but said nothing. Will started to pick up the meat.

"My son-in-law is among the colonial volunteers," his father continued in the same quiet voice. "We want him and the other soldiers to have the best food available."

The colonial officer coughed and cleared his throat. "We won't be needing the meat after all."

Will set it back with a quick, silent prayer of thanks.

"My family and I are grateful for your kindness, officers. In return, perhaps you will join us for dinner before you leave? My wife made apple pies fresh yesterday."

Will could hardly believe his ears. These men had almost cleaned out their winter food stores, and his father was offering them something to eat!

The officers eagerly accepted his offer and followed him to the dining room. In the kitchen, the British officer grabbed onions and rings of dried apples and pumpkins that hung on linen threads from the rafters. He handed them to Will and Tim, indicating they should take them, too, to the wagon. Beth stared with her mouth hanging open. Mrs. Smith's lips pressed together firmly, but she said nothing.

The dining room was a beautiful room, filled with furniture Father and Grandfather had made. On the mantel was the set of scales Great-grandfather Phillip Smythe had used in his apothecary shop. *If the officers knew anything at all about craftsmanship, they were sure to be impressed,* Will thought.

His mother might not like the men taking her food, but Will knew she'd be proud to serve them in that room. He wondered if his father had suggested the meal just to give his mother a chance to feel she was doing them a service, rather than feel the victim of their high-handed raiding—even if such action had been sanctioned by Governor Dudley.

When the family was ready to sit down to dinner, Mr. Smith turned to Tim. "You may wait for me in the parlor."

Will watched him eye the pie hungrily. "Yes, sir."

His father laid a hand on Tim's shoulder. "I expect you to be there when I come to you."

Tim's face grew pale beneath his brown curls. His fingers curled to clench his long vest. "Y. . .yes, sir."

Will was glad he hadn't gone with Jeremy to watch the race.

That evening when Will and his father were alone, he asked, "Father, about the officers today—you didn't act very upset when they took all our food."

"They didn't take it all."

"They took a good deal of it. I thought Mother would cry."

"She's a strong woman. Besides, she knows the troops need

food for their journey. It takes a great amount of food to feed two thousand men."

"But I thought you and Mother didn't approve of the war or the soldiers."

"It's true we don't like war. Before you were born, during King Phillip's War, I fought with the colonial soldiers against the French. I saw many young men I knew from Boston die. Many young women like Mary were left widows, and many children lost their fathers. Your mother and I lost friends. Some of our friends lost limbs in the war and have had difficulty supporting themselves and their families."

"Then why did you give our food away without complaint?"

"The soldiers need it. Rob will need it. You know the reasons for the war. The raids on the merchant ships and fishing ships must stop. They are ruining our livelihood and often taking lives. Along the wilderness border, the French continue to raid the villages, destroying homes and taking lives, as they did with Rob's family."

He sighed deeply. "Sometimes war is necessary, but I wish it weren't. The American colonies include a huge amount of land. I wish the settlers here from every country could live together in peace, instead of trying to grab each other's trade."

"Then you do believe we should revenge ourselves on the French?"

Mr. Smith hesitated. He picked up the Bible from the table beside him and rubbed one scarred hand over the cover. "The Bible says that only the Lord has the right to seek revenge. He tells us we are to forgive those who harm us."

"Is there a difference between revenge and defending our trade and our lives?"

"I think so. Sometimes, when we've been hurt by another, it's hard to know if there's a difference. We want revenge, whether it is necessary or not." He set the Bible down and slipped an arm across Will's shoulders. "Come, let's see what your mother and Beth are doing."

Though he walked along with his father, Will couldn't stop thinking about their conversation. He couldn't argue with the Bible. Nor could he help but feel the Bostonians were right for wanting to avenge the hardships and deaths caused by the French over the years. *How could people forgive such things?* he wondered.

CHAPTER TWELVE

Will Gets Caned

September 18, 1710

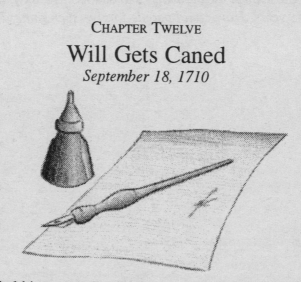

Will pulled his coat more tightly about him and leaned against the side of the small, two-masted ship. He'd forgotten the late September wind would be so chill off the waters.

He could hardly believe he was here! At first his father had said he and Beth had to go to school instead, but they'd finally convinced him the entire family should have a chance to say this good-bye to Rob. Even though Rob probably couldn't even see them in the little ketch, he'd know they were out there among all the boats.

Will's gaze was glued to the five warships ahead of them and the more than thirty transports and ketches that accompanied the men-of-war, carrying men and provisions to the St. Lawrence River—and to battle. He'd counted thirty ships with sails and several open sloops carrying bulky stores. Which ship carried Rob?

The *Dragon,* the warship he'd visited with General Nicholson, was leading the fleet. The general had left days ago to meet the land troops. Captain Martin was in charge of the *Dragon.*

Will tried to imagine being aboard it now as one of the marines. What must it feel like to be headed into battle? Did excitement race through the soldiers' veins as it did through his at the thought of what was ahead?

In addition to the fleet, the bay was filled with smaller boats of every shape. The Smiths were among many Bostonians who had left their work to see the men off. Those piloting the boats had to be careful to avoid hitting each other. The bay was so full that Will thought with a chuckle that he could almost walk from one boat to another all the way to land.

Hundreds of seagulls from their homes on the bay's rocky islands filled the sky as if they, too, were giving the fleet a send-off. He could hear their cries above the waves slapping against the hull and the wind that tore at him.

The ketch leaped against a wave. A spray of saltwater hit him in the face when the boat crashed down in the swell after the wave. Will caught hold of a rope attached to the side of the ship to keep his balance. Beside him, Mary slipped and fell against him heavily. He steadied her with his free arm.

She straightened herself, her cape whipping free in the wind. She stared into the breeze, never taking her gaze from the ships. Tears ran over her cheeks in a steady stream, but at least she wasn't sobbing anymore. It seemed to Will that she hadn't stopped crying since Robert had left to join the troops yesterday afternoon.

Rob had been allowed only a short time away from the ship yesterday. Like the other soldiers, he'd had to help with last minute preparations. He'd joined the family in the evening, spending a few minutes alone with each member, saying good-bye.

He'd spent most of his time with Mary. She'd even walked down to the wharf with him, where he joined other troops in the sloop that carried the soldiers out to the larger ships. She'd stayed at their house last night. She said the small rooms she and Rob lived in above their father's cabinetmaker's shop were too quiet without Rob.

"Cheer up, Mary. He won't be gone long."

She darted him a watery look. "We don't know that."

"Look at all those ships. They're carrying almost two thousand men! Surely you don't think the French can destroy them."

"Rob is only one man."

"He's one of the colonials' best marksmen. Not much chance anything will happen to him. It's the enemy who'd best watch out for him, not vice versa."

She gave him a shaky smile and brushed at the trail of tears with her fingertips. "Rob is a fine soldier, I know. I just miss him, and I. . .I don't want anything to happen to him."

"No one wants anything to happen to him. Least of all Rob. I'm sure he'll be careful."

"Yes." She didn't sound too sure.

Will decided to try another road to cheering her up. "Wasn't it good of Father to rent space for all of us on this ketch so we could follow the fleet as it departed?"

"I wish we could follow it all the way!" She grasped the edge of the board along the top of the shoulder-high side of the boat and stared at the fleet. "I feel so helpless, standing here watching Rob sail away from me."

"I wish I were going with him. If I were old enough, I would have volunteered, too."

Mary reached an arm out and rested it on his shoulders, her cloak forming an unexpected and welcome barrier against the winds. "I wish I could have volunteered, too."

Will swallowed a laugh. As if girls would ever be soldiers! "You would have had to learn how to fire a musket."

She smiled at him—a weak little smile, but a smile. "Yes, I guess I would have had to at that."

At least she was trying to cheer up. It was a start.

They were at the edge of the channel now, where the ocean met the outgoing waters powerfully. The waves grew stronger, and Will and the others had to brace their feet against the floorboards and hang on tighter to keep from being tossed around.

The boat began to turn about, and Will saw other boats turning, too. They were heading back. He looked over his shoulder as they turned, disappointment washing away his earlier excitement. He watched the distance increase between their boat and the last of the fleet until he couldn't see them anymore.

"Godspeed," he whispered into the wind.

The next few days Boston seemed strangely quiet. The streets were empty without the extra colonials and British troops. The town's craftsmen were busy in their shops, working on their usual orders instead of items for the military. Even the wharf was quiet. The harbor looked empty without the fleet's transports and sloops.

Boring, Will thought in surprise. After the hurry of preparing for the Port Royal expedition, Boston was boring. He'd never before considered the largest town in the colonies uninteresting.

He ran up the stairs to the second-story schoolroom. The day had been mild, but his hair was damp with sweat from the mock battle he and the other boys had just finished. The boys had gathered at Mill Pond at noon every day this week. They'd divided up into two "armies," one pretending to be the French, the other the British and colonials. Since he and Jeremy were two of the oldest boys, the others had chosen them to play the leaders. No one truly wanted to be the French, of course, so the armies traded—one day they would be French, the next, British.

Today, Will's group had the honor of being British and colonial. They'd whipped Jeremy's French army well.

He stood in a friendly tangle with his army for a minute, laughing with them as they relived the final moments of the battle, then took his seat.

Jeremy stalked across the room. Will brushed his damp hair from his forehead and grinned at him. Jeremy glared back, dropped onto the bench beside him, and crossed his arms over his chest.

Will felt his grin fade. Jeremy hadn't gotten any friendlier lately. "It was just a pretend battle," he said.

Jeremy's bottom lip jutted out in a pout. Not only didn't he answer Will, he didn't even look at him.

"Your army fought well, Jeremy. General Nicholson would be glad to have you for one of his officers." He nudged Jeremy playfully with his elbow.

Jeremy scuttled a few inches farther down the bench.

As Mr. Evans took his place at the front of the room, calling the class to order, Will sighed. Life lost a lot of its fun when his best friend acted like his enemy. Anyone would think they were really on opposite sides of the war.

The afternoon started with prayer, as always. Today Joshua was chosen to pray. He asked God to give the officers of the Port Royal expedition wisdom in battle and to keep the British and colonial troops safe. Every prayer at the school since the fleet had sailed had included that request, as had all the prayers at Will's home.

No matter how hard he tried, Will couldn't concentrate on his schoolwork that afternoon. The younger boys were reading their daily assignment aloud—all of them at once, as was normal. Mr. Evans interrupted them occasionally to correct them if someone didn't pronounce a word correctly. Will used to wonder how he could hear an individual in that noise and know who made the mistake. Now he was so used to hearing them recite, that he could hear the mistakes himself and know who the unfortunate lads were who made them.

It wasn't the reciting that distracted him today. He just couldn't stop thinking about Rob and the fleet. It had been five days since they sailed. They should be at Port Royal soon.

He stared out the window, imagining the fleet arriving at the fort on the wide St. Lawrence. The quill in his hand stopped its scratching across the parchment. Once the fleet arrived, how soon before they began firing on the fort? Would they wait until the French fired on them before lighting the massive cannons he'd seen on board the *Dragon*?

He could imagine what it would be like in battle with the roar of the many huge black cannons he'd seen on the *Dragon*, blazes of orange shooting from their mouths, the ships rocking from the cannons' recoil. Rolls of smoke from the cannons would almost hide the fort from the ships.

What must Rob be feeling if they'd reached the fort? Excitement? Fear? Surely not that last, not a marksman as good as Rob.

"Master William!"

Mr. Evans's voice jerked Will's attention back to Boston. The schoolmaster shook his head, pointed to the quill dangling in Will's hand, and turned back to the readers.

Will glanced down at his paper. A big black ink blot spread

across the otherwise neat page. He'd best keep his mind on his writing. The blot meant he'd be scored poorly for this afternoon's work.

But his mind wouldn't stay where he ordered it. The readers completed their recitation and went on to quieter work. Will watched idly as Mr. Evans sat down at his desk, opened the large journal he kept there, uncapped his ink bottle, and dipped his quill into it.

When he touched the quill's tip to his page, he frowned. He picked up the quill, looked at its tip, then touched his finger to it. Even from across the room, Will could see the ink came off in a thick glob. He bit back a chuckle. The schoolmaster would have a blot on his own work today.

Mr. Evans scowled down at his finger, then rubbed the blob between his finger and thumb. The scowl deepened. He lifted his fingers to his long, thin nose and sniffed. Will watched, curious. What was he doing?

The schoolmaster's hand came down on his desk in a fist. Thud! All eyes in the room turned to him. His thin lips pressed together so hard they couldn't have been tighter if sewn together. His face was fiery red.

"Which of you put molasses in my inkwell?"

Will hadn't known the old man could roar so loudly. If the schoolmaster hadn't been so furious, Will would have laughed. But he knew better than to laugh at a man when he was as angry as Mr. Evans was at this minute.

Some of the younger boys hadn't learned that lesson yet. Their giggles brought another roar from the master. "Silence!"

The laughing stopped.

Mr. Evans stood slowly, leaning his weight on the fists on his desk. "The only sound I want to hear from any of you is the answer to my question. Who put the molasses in my inkwell?"

No one spoke. Only the shuffle of nervous feet broke the silence. Will almost thought he could hear the sand running through the hourglass on the master's desk.

"Very well," Mr. Evans said, "since none of you is man enough to confess, I shall have to search you."

He began with the older boys. *Evidently he believes the younger boys unlikely of such a prank,* Will thought, *and he's probably right. Most likely it was Jeremy again. Just the kind of trick he'd pull.*

But when Jeremy emptied all his pockets at the schoolmaster's command, there was nothing to indicate that he was the culprit. Mr. Evans examined Jeremy's hands carefully, but there was only a bit of dirt on them from their noon battle. The master gave Jeremy a long, grave look before moving on to Will.

Will held out his hands before the schoolmaster could demand it. He had nothing to hide. When the man nodded his satisfaction, Will started pulling things out of his pockets and laying them beside the blotted paper.

Mr. Evans caught his breath in a gasp and grabbed Will's arm. Will started in surprise. The master jerked at his sleeve.

"Molasses!"

Will stared at his wide woolen sleeve in disbelief. There on the back above the elbow was a swipe of brown about an inch wide. How had it gotten there?

His stomach felt like something was slithering through it. He was in trouble again for something he hadn't done—again.

Mr. Evans's grasp on his arm tightened. He started toward the front of the room in a jerking gait, dragging Will with him. The cane in one wrinkled hand struck the wooden floor in an angry beat with every other step.

At the front of the room, the schoolmaster stuck his narrow face only inches away from Will's. "I'm disappointed in you

85

William Smith. Until the last few months, you were one of the best students I've had in all my years of teaching. As one of the eldest students, you've a duty to present a good example to the others. Instead, one would think you've appointed yourself the instructor of pranks."

"Sir, I—"

"I've not given you permission to speak."

"But I didn't do it, sir."

The man jerked the material on Will's sleeve back and forth. "This proves otherwise. You shall be responsible for splitting the classroom's firewood for a week."

"But, sir—"

"In addition, should your shenanigans prove to be such a disturbance that anyone fails their lesson today, you shall take their punishment."

Fury boiled inside Will as he took his seat on the bench behind the slanted desk. He ignored the glances from the other boys and went to work. He gripped his quill so hard that he couldn't form proper smooth loops.

Toward the end of the day he began to relax. Most of the boys had done well on their lessons. But Jeremy's ciphering was awful; he added only a few of his sums correctly.

Will watched Mr. Evans's face while Jeremy stumbled through his lesson. Dread grew larger inside his chest with each mistake. He wasn't surprised when Mr. Evans announced Jeremy's failing score and ordered Will to the front of the room again. Will threw back his shoulders and lifted his chin as he walked to the desk.

"Hold out your hand."

Will felt the blood drain from his face. He was going to have his hand beaten. He'd seen it happen to other students—not often, but a few times. It had never happened to him. There'd never been a cause.

Slowly he extended his hand, palm up.

Mr. Evans lifted the wooden cane. "I hate to do this, lad. I'd not do it if it were your first offense, but lately you've grown too fond of pranks. You must learn such behavior is not acceptable."

The cane came down across his palm with a smack. Will sucked in a small breath. He hadn't realized it would sting so! Tears sprang to his eyes at the sudden pain. He opened his eyes wide to keep the tears from falling. He wouldn't give the true prankster the satisfaction of seeing him cry, no matter how much it hurt.

Smack! The cane fell again. And again.

He stopped counting the blows. He stared out at the class. Who had done this to him? Whose punishment was he taking?

His gaze searched the faces. Pity was all he saw on most of them. Pity! As if he wanted their pity.

There was no pity in Jeremy's eyes. Instead there was a smug smile on his round, freckled face. Was he so angry about losing the pretend battle today that he was glad to see his best friend punished? Was he the one who had put the molasses in the ink-well? Surely he hadn't failed his sums on purpose!

Smack!

Will gritted his teeth until they hurt. He was going to find out who the real prankster was, and when he did, he was going to pay him back but good!

CHAPTER THIRTEEN

Will Father Understand?

The day went from bad to worse. Will's hand throbbed with pain, and with every throb his anger grew toward the boy whose hand should have been whipped instead of his. Every time he looked at Jeremy's smug face, he grew more certain Jeremy was to blame for everything.

When school was out, he raced down the steps, his gaze searching for Jeremy. He saw him half a block away, hurrying in the direction of his father's shop.

Will soon caught up with him. He grabbed Jeremy's arm and swung him about. "You did it, didn't you!"

"Did what?"

"You know what. You put the molasses in old Evans's inkwell, purposely failed your lesson, and then sat there like you were a perfect angel and watched me take your punishment."

"You know I've always been poor at ciphering. Besides, you're the one with molasses on your sleeve."

"And you're the one who put it there."

"Prove it!"

Will lifted a fist, ready to jam it into Jeremy's round, freckled nose, when someone grabbed his arm. "Stop it, Will!"

Pesty Beth! He might have known. She was always trying to catch up with him after school so they could walk to the shop together. He shook off her hands. "Leave me alone, Beth."

"Father will whip you good when he finds out you've been fighting in the streets."

"We're not fighting." He glared at Jeremy. "Not yet, anyway." He plopped his fists on his hips and turned his anger on her. "And who is going to tell Father?"

Beth propped her own fists on her hips, stuck out her pointed chin, and glared back at him. "I will if you don't stop yelling at me."

She looked so funny trying to look like him—with her jaw shoved forward and her tiny fists pushed into the sides of her wide skirt—that Will would have laughed if he weren't still so mad.

"What are you fighting about?" she asked.

"Nothing."

Jeremy grinned. "I'll tell you." And he did. Will didn't stay to listen. He figured it wouldn't be the true version anyway. He started home, leaving Beth with his former friend.

By the time he got home, his hand was aching badly. He'd almost forgotten it when he confronted Jeremy. Now that his enemy wasn't there to yell at, the pain was back.

He only nodded at the men in the shop. He slipped into the back room and changed into his work clothes, looking at the molasses on his shirt with disgust. He'd have to try to wash it out without his parents seeing it.

Then he went into the backyard where there was a trough kept filled with water and stuck his hand in it. The water eased the pain a bit. He wished he could leave his hand in it for hours, but he knew his father would come looking for him if he didn't get back to the shop soon. Sighing, he dried his hand carefully against his leather apron and started inside.

He'd barely started sweeping when his father asked him to plane a small board for him.

Will walked slowly to the shelf where the planes were kept and selected one the right size. His stomach churned. Most days he was glad for a chance to work with wood, but not today with his injured hand.

Could he possibly use his left hand for the work? He tossed the idea away immediately. Likely he'd just gouge the wood, ruining it. That wouldn't please his father at all.

With his right hand, he grasped the wide chunk of wood that made up the plane and pressed it against the board, running it along the board's length. The metal in the middle of the plane bit into the wood as it should, peeling a thin layer of wood into a swirl of wood shaving.

The effort hurt his hand something fierce. He put his left hand on the back of the plane and covered it with his right hand. Maybe he could do it better that way. At least the blisters would be pressing against the skin of his other hand instead of the wood of the plane.

But he found he still couldn't do it without wincing.

What if his father saw him struggling? He darted a glance at him, only to find his father watching him with a puzzled frown.

"Is something wrong, son?"

It was on the tip of Will's tongue to say no, but he couldn't flat-out lie to his father. *Not telling him anything about that afternoon, hoping he could get by without his father finding out, might not be totally honest,* he thought, *but at least it wasn't a lie.*

But he dreaded telling him the truth. What if Father didn't believe he was innocent? Mr. Evans seemed willing enough to believe in Will's wrongdoing.

Will took a deep breath, walked over to his father, and held out his hand.

"Son!" His father grabbed Will's wrist in his large, callused hand. "What happened?"

His father's exclamation caught the attention of Charles and Tim. They gathered around to see what was wrong. Will wished they would leave. It was going to be bad enough telling his father without an audience.

He decided to ignore the others and looked straight into his father's brown eyes. He told his story in as few words as he could, eager to have it behind him. Telling it left him burning with fury all over again.

He could see anger in his father's eyes, too. It left a sinking feeling in his stomach.

"Let me see your shirt, son."

Why would he want that? Will wondered as he hurried to the back room to retrieve it.

His father studied the stain for only a moment. "This is on the back of your arm and high up. Is this the only stain?"

"Yes, sir."

"If you'd been the one to put molasses in the inkwell, you'd have been more likely to have molasses on the bottoms of your sleeve or on your shirt front. Mr. Evans should have realized that."

"Then you believe I didn't do it?"

Surprise filled his father's eyes. "Of course. You've never lied to me—at least, I'm aware of no lies."

A lump formed in Will's throat as he took back the shirt. He hadn't known before how important his father's trust was to him. It was almost worth the beating to find out his father believed in him.

"I'm sorry this happened to you, son. Unfair things happen to everyone in life. I suggest you be especially attentive and diligent in your schoolwork in the future, however, to avoid displeasing Mr. Evans further."

"Yes, Father. I wish I knew who did it."

Tim lifted the shirt sleeve and grinned. "I bet your mother will wish she knew, too, when she tries to get this sticky brown stuff off your shirt."

Will laughed. It felt so good, that he laughed even harder. A few minutes ago, he never would have thought he'd be able to laugh about this. Just went to show, nothing bad that happened had to make the rest of life bad.

Still, he was going to find a way to pay Jeremy back.

"Get some clean rags, son, and I'll bandage that hand for you."

"Yes, sir."

Will turned to go back to his work and almost tripped over the wooden cradle sitting on the floor. It rocked back and forth. He hurried around it and headed for the small room where rags were kept.

Rob had made the cradle for the baby he and Mary were expecting. He'd stolen hours from his noon breaks and worked long into the evening, sometimes past candle-lighting time, to finish it before he left.

Will had kept him company during some of those late hours. They'd talked about the war, the Deerfield raid in which Rob's family had been killed, the good life Rob hoped his baby would know. He'd volunteered as much for his baby as to revenge the family he'd lost.

"If we can win Queen Anne's War," he'd said, "and force the French to leave the American lands, maybe our baby won't have to fight in a war when he grows up or watch people he loves go off to war."

Will found the barrel filled with rags and pulled out a piece of linen. His thoughts stayed with Rob. Rob had told him he wanted to finish the cradle before he left, in case there wasn't time when he returned from Port Royal. Sometimes babies come earlier than expected, he'd reminded Will.

Rob wanted the cradle kept at the shop until the baby was born. It was a surprise for Mary.

Will glanced at the cradle again when he went back into the main shop. Was that the only reason Rob had been so determined to finish the cradle? Because the baby might arrive too soon?

Or was Rob afraid he might not come back from Port Royal?

The thought chilled Will to his bones, in spite of the warm September day. He'd never really considered the possibility that Rob might be killed. Or maimed. A carpenter from a shop down the street had lost an arm in a battle a few years ago. He wasn't a carpenter any longer. He couldn't do the work with only one arm.

Will shrugged his shoulders as if to push away the disturbing thoughts. He was getting as bad as Mary! Rob wouldn't be hurt. He couldn't be! Why, he'd be one of the bravest soldiers fighting for the colonials—and winning. In a couple months he'd be back from battle, and they'd laugh together over Mary's silly fears.

Besides, hadn't next Thursday been declared a day of fasting and prayer for the troops' success? All of Boston would be praying for their victory and safety.

Mr. Smith took the linen rag and waved a hand toward a wooden stool. "Sit down."

When Will was seated, his father knelt in front of him, his

leather-clad knees crunching the sawdust. His work-worn hands were gentle as they wrapped the linen about Will's red, blistered palm.

His father looked tired. Large gray circles were beneath his eyes. There were lines in his face Will hadn't noticed before.

Of course, Will thought, watching his father tie the bandage in a large knot. With Rob away fighting, it was difficult for his father to keep up with the work. Charles and Tim weren't yet skilled enough to take Rob's place. It hadn't helped that they'd all had to spend so much time on military orders.

And now his father was worried because Jeremy—or someone else—was framing Will for the pranks at school.

Mr. Smith stood up and patted Will on the shoulder. "You'd best be getting home. You can't do much work until your hand starts to heal."

"Yes, sir. Thank you."

His father smiled at him.

Will smiled back. He slipped off the stool and headed out the door, leaving behind the familiar wood scents for the street. A pleasant feeling settled in his chest. His father believed in him. He believed Will was honest, that he hadn't put the molasses in the inkwell, and that he was able to take care of the problem by himself. He hadn't embarrassed them both by saying so, but Will knew it was true.

He clenched his good hand into a fist at his side. It made him all the more determined to take revenge on the prankster.

CHAPTER FOURTEEN

The Schoolroom Battle
October 26, 1710

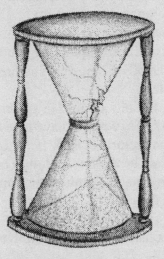

"Charge, men!" Jeremy called out.

His army let go from one side of the schoolroom with a shout. Twigs served for swords and muskets. Some still had a few dry autumn leaves hanging from them, others were bare. The boys waved their "weapons" in the air as they charged across the room.

"Fire, men!" Will ordered his army.

One line of his men dropped to one knee and fired their twig muskets. Then a second line fired as the first pretended to reload.

"I'm hit, I'm hit!"

"Ow!"

Some of the boys on each side grabbed parts of their bodies and stumbled about, pretending to be wounded. None would admit to having been killed.

Jeremy's army reached the first line of Will's army. They struck at branch muskets with wobbly twig swords. More wounded cries went up.

One of Jeremy's men grabbed an ink bottle and pretended it was a powder horn. He tipped it over the end of his branch as if filling a musket with powder.

"Don't!" Will cried.

Too late. The inkwell's cork plopped out. Black ink splashed down the front of the boy's long vest and breeches and puddled on the floor at his feet.

Will groaned. In trouble again! He glanced at the hourglass on the master's desk. They might have time to blot up the puddle before Mr. Evans returned from his noon meal, but they'd never get the stain out of the boy's clothes or the floorboard.

The rest of the boys hadn't noticed the spill. They were completely involved in their battle.

"Stop! Everyone stop!"

Will clenched his hands in frustration. No one paid him any attention.

George, the young boy who spilled the ink, stared at his shirt, then the floor, then at Will. His blue eyes filled with tears. Will remembered George was the youngest in the class.

He took the ink bottle from him, corked it, and set it down. "Go wash your hands. I'll try to clean up the puddle."

George had to dodge a number of fighting soldiers to make it to the class drinking bucket.

Will searched for a cloth and finally found one by the schoolmaster's desk. Before he could get back to the puddle, he heard Jeremy shout, "Man the cannons!"

A moment later a *New England Primer* whizzed past Will's ear. "Watch out for cannonballs!" Jeremy cried, tossing another book across the room.

"Not the schoolbooks!" *How could anyone treat a book like that?* Will wondered.

Shock rooted his shoes to the floor as others threw books at their "enemies," their imitations of booming cannons cutting off Will's attempts to stop them.

He dodged another book.

Crash!

The hourglass landed on the floor, sand and broken glass flying everywhere.

Crash!

A window!

"Stop!" Will raced around the desk and grabbed a book from a tall, skinny boy just as he was about to toss it. "Stop!" He grabbed for another textbook cannonball. Missed.

Why wouldn't they stop? He pushed his way to the middle of the room, urging everyone to quit playing.

He glanced over the heads and waving arms and branches. Mr. Evans! He was standing in the doorway leaning on his cane, his face filled with rage.

"Stop!" Will yelled at the top of his lungs.

No one stopped.

Will saw another primer fly out of Jeremy's hand. It landed smack on top of Mr. Evans's head, knocking his long white wig to the floor. The schoolmaster clapped a hand to his shaved head.

Jeremy stared at the master, his mouth hanging open as though he were a fish.

Mr. Evans shoved his wig back on with one hand. It sat crookedly on his head, almost covering one side of his face. He pounded his cane against the floor. "Order! I will have order!"

The battle cries died a sudden death.

Laughter broke the silence when the boys saw Mr. Evans's curls dangling about his nose.

"Silence!"

The boys stood where they were, twigs and books still in their hands.

Will's heart was beating like a drum. He watched Mr. Evans look slowly around the room. The man's face grew redder and his lips tighter as he looked from the sand and glass that used to be the hourglass to the broken window to the books scattered about the floor to the branches in almost every hand.

The other boys watched, too. Will saw them look at each other with panic on the faces that had been cheerfully calling war cries but a minute earlier.

Mr. Evans pinned his angry gaze on Jeremy. "Master Clark, what has been going on here?"

Will saw Jeremy swallow hard. "A. . .a b. . .battle, sir. The British against the French."

"A battle in my schoolroom?"

Jeremy's hands closed in a fist and opened again. "It's raining outside, sir."

"I'm aware of that. It will soon be raining inside, since the window's been broken."

The tip of Jeremy's tongue ran along his lips, as if they were dry. Will almost felt sorry for him, in spite of the trouble he'd caused Will lately. Almost, but not quite.

"Are you responsible for this battle, Master Clark?"

"In. . .in a way, sir. I'm captain of one of the armies."

"Who is the other captain?"

Will took a deep breath and stepped forward. "I am, sir."

Mr. Evans glared at him. "I might have known." He leaned against his desk, crossed his arms over his long black coat, and looked the class over. "I've never had cause to punish an entire class before. But rest assured each of you shall be punished. While I'm considering what punishment could possibly fit such a monstrous crime, you may all straighten the room."

Will and Joshua looked at each other. Joshua turned his back to the schoolmaster, bent the corners of his lips down, rolled his eyes, and knelt to pick up a book.

Will knew just how he felt. Mr. Evans could make all their lives miserable if he chose. Not that they didn't deserve it, he admitted to himself, reaching for a torn primer.

"May I ask the reason for the branches of which you all seem so fond?" Mr. Evans raised his eyebrows above still angry eyes.

The boys glanced at each other, rolling the branches they still held between their fingers. Will felt his face grow hot and knew it was as red as everyone else's. No one looked at Mr. Evans or answered him.

Finally Will said, "Weapons, sir."

Mr. Evans snorted and laughed. Will's face grew hotter.

"Pile the muskets and sabers by the door," the master demanded sarcastically. "Then you may take them outside, Master Clark."

When the room was finally brought to rights—leaves, pieces of twigs, glass, and sand swept up, books picked up from the floor and returned to their owners, branches outside—the students stood in front of their seats and awaited their punishment.

He walked back and forth in front of the class, eyeing the boys sternly, his cane keeping a steady beat as usual. "I can see

I shall have to—" He stopped in front of the ink spot on the floor. "Who is responsible for this?"

His gaze flickered across the class and rested on the young boy with black ink stains down his shirt and breeches. The lad started trembling. Will couldn't stand the thought of the youngster possibly receiving a painful switching for the accident.

"It's my fault, sir," he blurted out before he even realized he was going to say it.

Gratitude stared at him out of the youngster's big brown eyes. *Well,* Will thought, *he'd always heard officers were responsible for the behavior of the men under them.* He was already in trouble with the schoolmaster. What was a little more? But he didn't like to think what his father would say.

The schoolmaster stopped directly in front of Will and leaned on his cane with both hands. "Master Smith, what has happened to make you so unruly the last months?"

"I don't know, sir."

Mr. Evans turned away from him and addressed the rest of the class. "You shall all spend your noon times next week copying the small catechism. I expect your finished results will have no ink blots. In addition, since masters Smith and Clark have enjoyed serving as your captains, they or their fathers shall pay for a new window and hourglass."

Will bit the inside of his mouth. He exchanged a glance with Jeremy. Their fathers weren't going to be happy about this.

"As for the ink you spilled in your play, Master Smith—"

The schoolmaster stopped as if to be sure he had everyone's attention before announcing Will's extra punishment.

Will clasped his hands together behind his back and looked right into Mr. Evans's eyes.

George started forward. "Sir, he didn't—"

"Boom!" A cannon blast stopped the young boy's confession.

Everyone, including Mr. Evans, stared at the windows, punishments forgotten.

"Boom!"

Another blast. Warships had been sighted in the channel! Will's stomach lurched. Nicholson and Martin had taken all the shot from the fortlike areas called batteries that guarded North and South Boston, as well as that for the cannons recently placed at the Neck—the only way to reach Boston by land. If the warships weren't friendly, there wasn't any ammunition for the town's cannons, and very few armed soldiers were left in town to fight.

But it had been five weeks since the British marines and colonials had left for Port Royal. Could they be returning?

Will swung around to face Mr. Evans. The man's face was almost as white as his wig. "Could it be General Nicholson and the troops, sir?"

The schoolmaster's face regained a bit of color. "It most likely is."

Relief swept through the room like a breeze. Boys started whispering to each other eagerly, ending the dreadful, fear-filled silence that had crept over the room at the sound of the first cannon blast.

Drums began to beat, their sound coming in through the broken window along with the crisp October air. Drums that called the few remaining men of the town militia to arms in case the men-of-war belonged to the enemy or to form an honor guard if the ships were friendly.

Will's heart beat faster than the drums. Which would it be? In spite of the punishments for the noon battle, Will couldn't keep his attention on his schoolwork. When it was time for ciphering, he struggled through long sums that he usually solved with ease. His gaze constantly wandered to the window, wondering if sails billowed over General Nicholson's and Captain Martin's returning fleet in the harbor below.

The excitement of the cannons and drums must have shoved the thought of further punishment from the schoolmaster's mind for the moment, Will thought. Mr. Evans hadn't mentioned any punishments since the first cannon shot. Could it be the old schoolmaster was as excited over the possible return of the Port Royal expedition as the boys?

Will could hardly bear to wait any longer to see Rob. He wanted to hear all about the battles his brother-in-law had been in.

His gaze darted about the room. He wasn't the only one with a relative in the colonial forces. Joshua and Jeremy's older brothers were both with the troops. And the youngster who'd spilled the ink, his father had gone with the fleet. No wonder no one could concentrate on their schoolwork.

Mr. Evans was uncharacteristically inattentive, staring out the broken window, the autumn breeze rippling the white scarf tied so properly at his throat. Did he have friends or relatives among the troops, too? Will had never before thought of him as a regular person with a family and friends and a life outside the schoolroom. Was there someone special he was worried about?

Not that I'm worried about Rob, Will reminded himself hastily. Nothing could have happened to Rob.

CHAPTER FIFTEEN

Where's Rob?
October 26, 1710

"The fleet's returned! The fleet's returned!"

The news, yelled by a passerby running through the street, came through the broken schoolroom window like a trumpet.

The class burst into cheers. Smiles wreathed every face, chasing away the worry and doubt that had sat on them since noon.

Excitement beat through Will's veins.

The door burst open, and the shopkeeper from the first floor entered, his eyes shining. "Did you hear?" he demanded of Mr.

Evans. "The fleet's returned!"

Evans nodded.

The shopkeeper grinned, his thin lips almost meeting his ears. "Governor Dudley's called a town meeting for this afternoon. I hear tell it's good news."

The students broke into excited chatter, and Will couldn't hear anything more that passed between the men. When the shopkeeper left, Mr. Evans called the class to order.

"The governor, as you've just heard, has called a town meeting. Therefore, we shall dismiss for the day with prayer."

Will thought he'd never heard so many feet shuffling during a prayer as that afternoon. He knew everyone was as anxious to get to the town house as he was.

Still, he stopped at home to be certain his mother and Mary had heard the news. Beth was already there. The four of them hurried to the shop, and his father and the apprentices joined them.

Mary was trying to act calm, but Will thought she looked anxious. She kept biting her lips. Her gaze darted about the crowd gathered about the wooden pillars of the lower town house.

Banners hung from the town house's windows. Will's spirits soared. The shopkeeper must have been right. The governor must have received good news about the battle. The town house was only decorated with banners for special, happy occasions.

Soon there was barely room to move in the street. Shopkeepers bumped up against housewives, whose feet were stepped on by craftsmen, whose leather aprons and everyday dark jackets looked a bit shoddy beside merchants' fancy clothes, whose fancy clothes looked even fancier beside sailors' dirty, sweaty shirts and breeches. A fish vendor stood beside Will, and Will blinked at the stench of the man's wares.

The portly governor in his fine emerald green knee-length coat and fancy white waistcoat and breeches finally appeared on the captain's walk atop the building—the only place from which everyone could hear him. A moment later two officers joined him, one on each side. Will immediately recognized General Nicholson and Captain Martin.

The governor deliberately shoved the long curls of his white wig back from his shoulders and placed a large megaphone to his mouth. "Bostonians, the fleet has returned from Port Royal. Our men return in victory!"

Shouts and hats filled the air. Women hugged their husbands and children. Men slapped each other on the back and grinned and told each other they'd known the British and colonials would win. Beth threw her arms around Will's neck. For a minute Will forgot where they were and hugged her back. But only for a minute.

He noticed Mary had her arms around Father's neck. She was crying again, but this time she was crying because she was happy. Or at least, he figured she must be happy because she was smiling a huge smile, even while tears rolled over her cheeks and dampened their father's work shirt.

Mary let go of their father and looked at Will with a mischievous twinkle in her eyes. Before he knew what was happening, she was hugging him.

He felt silly with her hanging on him like that, but he didn't push her away like he had Beth. He was so glad to see her happy again, he would have let her hug him if they'd been standing on the captain's walk with the governor and officers. If he was relieved the soldiers were back, how much more relieved must she be?

The governor's voice, amplified by the megaphone, finally caught the crowd's attention. Mary quit hugging him, and the crowd quieted enough for the governor to continue. After a word or two, he handed the megaphone to General Nicholson.

"We had an easy victory over Port Royal," he announced. "One of the easiest victories in the history of warfare."

The crowd let loose with another roaring cheer.

After a few minutes Nicholson held up a hand, and the crowd quieted again. In a few short sentences, the general told how Port Royal had been overtaken. "There were very few casualties," he said. "One small boat of British marines capsized trying to land on the rocky shoreline. Twenty-six of those marines died. Only a handful of colonials and British were killed setting up batteries for our troops to use in their attack. The mission was a resounding success. Port Royal has been renamed Annapolis Royal in honor of England's Queen Anne."

"Hurrah for Queen Anne!" someone in the crowd called out.

"Hurrah for Nicholson and Martin!" the fish vendor beside Will yelled.

The cry was taken up by the rest of the crowd. Will yelled along with the rest, barely noticing that Beth again had hold of his arm to steady herself while she jumped up and down and screamed cheers at the top of her lungs.

Governor Dudley took the megaphone again. The crowd waited eagerly. "I proclaim this a day of thanksgiving to God for the victory and for the safety of our men. The ministers of the town's four churches will hold services of thanksgiving this evening. Two hundred and fifty of our men remained at the fort at Annapolis. The remaining Massachusetts men are now coming ashore."

Mary started pushing through the crowd toward the wharves. After his first surprise, Will joined her. Soon most of the town was headed toward the docks.

There was no telling at which of the many long docks or wharves Rob would land. Like so many others from the town square, Will and Mary headed straight down King Street and out on Long Wharf. It was the newest wharf in town and not even completed yet. It was wide enough for counting houses and warehouses to be built along one side, room for unloading ships on the other, and a lane for carts down the middle. By the time Will and Mary arrived, every inch of space was taken up with townspeople, sailors, and returning soldiers.

It seemed to Will that the harbor was filled with boats filled with soldiers. He was sure there were soldiers landing at every wharf. He took hold of Mary's elbow to get her attention and yelled into her ear, "We'll never find Rob in this mob."

But she didn't stop looking for him, so Will didn't, either. They watched boat after boat unload the happy returning soldiers. No Rob.

Will noticed a soldier grab a boy in a bear hug and realized it was the youngster who'd spilled the ink earlier that day. He was glad the boy's father had returned safe.

Mary occasionally stopped a soldier she knew and asked about Rob. No one knew which ship he was on.

"Maybe Rob stayed at Port Royal," Will finally suggested. "I mean Annapolis."

Mary shook her head vigorously. "He would never have volunteered to stay. Not with the baby coming."

Will had almost forgotten about the baby. It wasn't expected until early January, two-and-a-half months away. He remembered the cradle and thought Mary was most likely right. Rob would want to be home when the baby was born.

A queasy feeling started in his stomach. What if Rob had been wounded? But the general had said hardly any colonials had been killed or wounded. Surely a good soldier like Rob wouldn't have been injured.

"We may as well wait for Rob at home, Mary. He could have already landed at another wharf and be at home waiting for you right now."

She flashed him a brilliant smile and they turned to leave the wharf. They couldn't walk very fast with all the people still about.

They passed Jeremy's father's cooper shop and house on the way home. Jeremy's older brother—the one who had challenged the British marines to the horse race the Sunday before the fleet sailed—was standing in front of the shop talking with his family and neighbors. Will waved at him and he waved back. But Jeremy looked the other way. Will knew he was only pretending he hadn't seen him.

Will and Mary stopped at their own father's shop on the way home. Mary and Rob lived over the shop, but Rob wasn't there and their father hadn't seen him.

"He's probably gone directly to Mother and Father's house," Mary said as they hurried away from the shop down the paved street toward the north end of town. "Surely he'd know I couldn't bear to wait for him alone. Besides, he'd want to see everyone."

"Sure," Will agreed. He hoped she was right.

But Rob wasn't at the house, either. By candle-lighting time, he still hadn't arrived.

The rest of the family quietly kept Mary company. Beth sat at a small table diligently copying a piece from the Bible by the light of a bayberry candle. Mother sat in a straight-backed chair beside the fire working patiently on a piece of needlework, as she so often did in the evenings. Father sat on the other side of the fire with a book by the Reverend Cotton Mather in his lap.

To look at all of them, it could have been any night of the year, Will thought. *No one would know they were waiting to hear the door open and Rob's cheerful, booming voice greet them.*

Will pretended to tend the evening fire in the parlor while he watched Mary. She'd put on her best dress—red and white with long lace hanging from the sleeves. She stood at the window, looking out between the long drapes that were a slightly deeper yellow than the walls. She wasn't smiling anymore, he noticed.

"There were almost a thousand Massachusetts men with the expedition," he reminded her. "It takes a long time to bring that many men to shore."

She gave him a stiff little smile and nodded.

A knock at the door sent her flying across the parlor, the wide smile of that afternoon back, lighting her brown eyes with joy.

Will and Beth started after her, but their father stopped them with a word and a shake of his head. "Let them have a couple minutes alone to say hello. Time enough for the rest of us to speak with him afterward."

Beth was even more impatient than he was, Will realized. She stood on tiptoe, stretching her skinny neck in an attempt to see around the parlor door into the entryway.

A man's deep voice carried into the parlor. Will's heart seemed to stop. It wasn't Rob's voice. It was General Nicholson's.

Mary led the great man into the parlor, a frightened look on her face. The skin on Will's arms and the back of his neck prickled. Why would the great man be at their house tonight? He should be celebrating his victory with the governor and selectmen.

Will's father rose to greet the general. Nicholson removed his hat and bowed slightly. He smiled at Will. "Good evening, friend."

Will smiled back, though he didn't feel like smiling inside. Something was wrong. Had Rob been injured after all? Maybe he hadn't come home because he was with the wounded. There were so many things he wanted to ask, but he only said, "Good evening, General. Congratulations on your victory."

"Thank you, lad."

Mary slipped to her father's side, sliding her hands through his arm, and stared at the general with a white face.

"Have you met my sister?" Will asked the general. "This is Mary Allerton, Rob's wife."

The important man turned to Mary with the gentlest look Will had ever seen in his eyes. "Then it is you I've come to see."

Mary made a funny little noise in her throat. Their father laid a hand over hers. The fire crackled and popped cheerfully.

"I'm sorry to inform you that your husband died in battle."

Danger at Mill Pond
December 1710

Will swung the heavy axe in an arc and brought it down on the upturned log with a loud thud. The metal bit into the wood. He pried it loose and swung again.

It soothed some of the anger inside him to chop wood. He'd been angry since he'd heard about Rob. He was glad there was something he could hit without getting in trouble.

He wiped the sweat from his brow with his brown wool shirt sleeve. The weather was mild for December. December. It had been two months since they'd found out Rob had died—the worst two months of his life.

Boston's rejoicing over the victory had lasted all through the night they heard of Rob's death and for days afterward. The cheerful crowds had hurt. How could the world go on as usual? How could adults go about their business and children go to school? Didn't they know the Smiths' lives had changed forever?

General Nicholson had tried to comfort them by reminding them how much the victory meant to Boston and the rest of New England. Rob was a hero, he'd said.

But the war wasn't over. The Port Royal expedition had been only one battle. Merchant ships, travelers, and fishermen were still not safe from the French when sailing the waters off New England. The towns and farmers on the frontier weren't safe, either. Nicholson had left Boston for London to ask the queen for more warships and more marines to continue the fight.

Thud! The metal bit into the wood again, spraying chips about him. *Rob might be a hero, but that didn't stop the pain of missing him,* Will thought.

"I wondered where you went." Beth lifted her blue skirt and stumbled toward him over the wood chips. "I thought you were going to help us finish packing Mary's things."

"Do you think I'm trying to avoid helping Mary move back home?" He wasn't. He was glad to have something he could do to help her for a change. It made him feel so helpless, knowing she was hurting because of Rob and knowing there wasn't anything he could do to make her feel better. "Father wants the wood chopped before I go back to school for the afternoon."

"You needn't get angry with me." Beth plopped down on a pile of wood, her wide skirt poufing out about her like a pretty blue cloud against the rough brown bark. "You're angry all the time lately."

He ignored her and swung the axe again. Thud! Why didn't

she just leave him alone?

He screwed his eyebrows into a scowl and darted a glance at her. She'd changed, too, in the last couple months. She wasn't the perky, chattering girl she'd been before Rob died. Now she was quiet, always watching Mary with wide, sad eyes.

Anyway, why shouldn't he be angry? He used to think life would be pretty good if he did the things that were expected of him, the things that were right, like learning his lessons well, doing his errands around the shop and at home, and obeying his parents.

Instead he was still being falsely accused of pranks at school, he missed Rob, he couldn't stop Mary from missing Rob, and he didn't know enough about cabinetmaking yet to step into Rob's place in his father's business. There was nothing in his life he could fix or control. Naturally he was angry! But Beth was just a little girl. How could she understand the way a boy felt about things?

Beth wrapped her arms around her knees and leaned against them, watching him. "The goldsmith told Martha's mother that they have to leave their rooms by the end of the month."

Martha's father had been killed in the battle, too, Will remembered. Mr. Lankford had been a journeyman goldsmith. He'd worked for a goldsmith down by Scarlett's Wharf, and his family had lived in rooms above the shop. He was sorry about Martha's father. Martha wasn't anything like Beth. She had reddish hair and freckles, and she'd always been quiet and reserved compared to bouncy Beth. He rather liked her, as much as any girl, that is.

Martha had a brother, Sam, who'd been born right before Nicholson returned from London last July with the men-of-war. Back then, Samuel and Martha had had a father, and their mother and Mary had had husbands. He couldn't imagine what it must be like not to have a father. He swung the axe again, as hard as he could.

"The goldsmith told Mrs. Lankford that since her husband didn't work for him anymore, they couldn't stay in his rooms."

"Where does he expect them to stay? They haven't any relatives here to live with, and Mrs. Lankford doesn't make any money."

"They're going to stay here, upstairs in the rooms Mary and Rob lived in."

He looked at her in surprise.

"I told Mary about them," she continued, "and she asked father if they might stay there. He said Mrs. Lankford can earn some of the rent by feeding his apprentices."

He should be glad for them, and for Beth. Instead bitterness ate away at his insides like a stomachache after he'd eaten too many green apples. Why couldn't he find ways to help people, instead of just feeling bad for them?

"Martha says her mother is trying to find a place to work. They can't afford for Martha to go to school anymore." Beth's blue eyes glinted with a hint of tears.

"I'm sorry, Beth. I know you'll miss seeing her every day."

Like he missed Jeremy, but Jeremy was still sitting next to him in class. They just weren't friends anymore.

"She'll have to watch Samuel while her mother works."

He didn't say anything. What could he say that would make any difference?

"I miss Rob. Do you miss him, Will?"

Will picked up another log, avoiding looking at her. "Course I do." Didn't do any good to talk about it that he could see. "Stand up and stick out your arms. You can help me carry in some wood."

She did as he asked, and he piled a few small pieces of firewood in her arms. She heaved a sigh so big it seemed to come from the hem of her skirt. "I wish I knew a way to make Mary feel better."

He looked at her, startled. Did she feel as helpless as he did inside? He opened his mouth to say something. Changed his mind and shut it. Changed his mind again and blurted out, "I'm starting to forget what he looks like. I wish he'd had his portrait painted, like the rich people do."

"Yes." A smile formed slowly on her narrow face.

"Now what are you thinking?"

"You gave me an idea. I'm going to draw a picture of Rob for Mary."

If anyone else had said that, he would have laughed, but Beth drew well. She was always sketching small pictures when she was supposed to be practicing her writing in the evenings. "Can you remember how he looked?" he asked.

"I think so. After I draw it, will you tell me if it looks like him?"

"Sure." *If I can remember,* he thought.

She started toward the back door of their father's shop with her load of wood, tripping over her skirt.

Will shook his head. Beth might not be as bubbly as before, but she hadn't changed completely. She was still as clumsy as ever. He couldn't imagine that she'd ever be as graceful as their sister Mary.

Grabbing some logs, he followed her inside. He'd dropped the logs beside the fireplace and was brushing chips of wood and bark from his brown wool shirt when his father said, "Will you help me carry the cradle Rob made out to the cart? The baby's birthing time is getting close. Besides, Mary hasn't seen it yet. Perhaps it will make her feel better to have something Rob made."

Will pulled the cradle out from beneath the worktable where

115

his father had stored it and pulled back the old piece of cloth that protected it. *How could a piece of wood Rob had worked on make Mary miss him any less?* he wondered.

He rubbed his hand over the cradle's bonnet, the same way he'd seen Rob do many times while he worked on it. The wood was smooth as cream. Rob must have put a lot of love into it. Will blinked back the salty tears that suddenly stung his eyes.

"Rob was a good man." His father's voice came from behind Will's shoulder. "I miss him."

Will didn't say anything. He was afraid that if he tried to speak he'd cry, so he just kept staring at the cradle.

"Learning to live with the pain of losing people who are killed in battle is one of the prices of war," his father continued quietly. "It's a pain that doesn't end with a victory or a peace treaty." He picked up the back end of the cradle. "Let's bring Mary her gift."

Will leaned over to pick up the other end, grateful his father had changed the subject. He didn't want to talk about his pain.

After they'd put the cradle with the other items in the one-wheeled wooden cart, Will hurried back inside the shop to wash his hands before going back to school for the afternoon. He used to enjoy going to school. Now he dreaded it. He never knew when he walked through the schoolroom door what he'd be blamed for before the day was over. The anger that had become such a part of him boiled over.

He couldn't do anything about Rob or the war. But he was going to find a way to get back at Jeremy for all those pranks at school. His father's reminder that revenge belongs to God and that Christians are to forgive their enemies slipped into his mind. He shoved the thought away.

He bumped against a small pile of stiff dried animal skins. Tim would be using them tomorrow to make glue they needed in the shop.

116

Glue. He smiled. A warm feeling of satisfaction filled him. Maybe he had a way to get back at Jeremy.

Three weeks later, on a mild January day, Will stood at Mr. Evans's desk in the empty schoolroom. Finally he'd had the chance to put his plan for revenge into action.

He listened carefully, barely breathing. Was that a footfall on the stairs? No. His breath whooshed out in relief. Everyone else had left for the two-hour noon break. He'd left with them, then circled through an alley and hurried back. He glanced at the new hourglass on the schoolmaster's desk. Unless someone came back unexpectedly, he had all the time in the world. And he only needed a couple minutes.

He opened the small flannel bag he'd had tied all morning to his waist beneath his black wool coat and removed a small pot. He pulled out the cork and dipped a twig inside. Flipping open one of Mr. Evans's books, he hesitated. It would be hard to do what he planned. He had such respect for books. But it was a great plan for getting Jeremy in trouble.

He took a deep breath and spread glue on a number of the pages. Then he closed the book, put both hands on the cover, and leaned on it with all his weight. There! The deed was done.

He tried to ignore the feeling of shame that squirmed across his chest and the words "forgive your enemies" that insisted on ringing in his ears. Hastily, he stuck the small covered pot back in his flannel bag and tied the bag back beneath his coat. He hurried over to Jeremy's seat and stuck the stick full of glue inside the cover of Jeremy's book.

At the door he paused for one last look around the room. Had he forgotten anything that would incriminate him? Nothing. Turning, he raced down the stairs.

He wanted to race through his meal of porridge and apple cider so he could hurry back, but Beth chose that time to give Mary the drawing she'd made of Rob. Will had to admit Beth had done a good job. He hadn't thought he remembered what Rob looked like, but he'd recognized Rob's face as soon as he'd seen the pen and ink drawing.

Beth had wanted to give the drawing to Mary as soon as it was done, but he convinced her the paper needed to be protected. He'd made a frame from black walnut. It had felt good to do something nice for Mary.

Mary was thrilled when she saw the drawing. Tears glistened on her eyelashes as she hugged Beth and then Will. "It looks just like Rob! And the frame is beautiful. I'll treasure this always."

A pleasant warmth spread through his chest at her words.

A few minutes later when he stopped by Mill Pond, he couldn't help but grin in anticipation of that afternoon. For once, he wasn't going to be the one in trouble before the end of the day.

A number of boys were already at Mill Pond, playing battle as was their practice. They never seemed to tire of it. The winter so far had been mild—there wasn't even any ice on the river or pond yet—so they'd been able to play about the pond in spite of the season.

At first, after Rob had been killed, Will hadn't had the heart to join in. But as his anger grew, he looked forward to the noon battles. He'd pretend it was the Port Royal battle and he was fighting alongside Rob. Only this time, Rob wasn't killed.

Today Jeremy had beaten him to Mill Pond and was leading his soldiers against the group that made up Will's army. Jeremy saw him arrive and smiled his usual smug smile.

"Just you wait," Will said under his breath, waving and pasting a friendly smile on his face. "You're about to get yours." He joined his group, whipping out the thin board from his father's shop that he'd shaped into a play sword.

Joshua, Will's second in command, and a few other boys had found some deadfall branches and tied them together into a raft a few days earlier. Jeremy's army couldn't stand the thought of Will's army having equipment they didn't. Today, Will saw, both armies had rafts.

The rafts weren't easy to stand on. Will knew, because he'd tried it himself a few times. The round, unpeeled logs made uneven footholds. To make matters worse, rope was the only thing that kept the logs together. As the boys jumped about on the raft, the logs would move apart as far as the wet ropes allowed, then smack together when a small wave hit them wrong.

Not that it was dangerous. They were only out a few feet from the mucky shoreline. Those who couldn't swim could walk to shore through the reeds when they fell off—or were knocked off by the enemy. They might catch a chill from the cold winter water, but that was all.

He stood on shore, cheering his marines on as the two rafts banged against each other on the gray water. About half the class was on land, and a dozen or so boys stood on the overcrowded rafts.

Will's attention was caught by an attack from some of Jeremy's men. He fought them off bravely with his wooden sword. He'd just managed to push the largest back onto his heavily padded bottom when he heard the screaming start.

It wasn't like the battle yells. This was different. It was high and shrill, and the terror in it sent goose bumps racing along his arms and neck.

He swung around to the pond where the screams came from. His scalp prickled. The rafts had drifted farther out in the water than usual. They were almost twenty feet from shore. George,

119

the young boy who had spilled ink on the floor, was lying face down in the water. A stream of red lay along the top of the water by his head.

CHAPTER SEVENTEEN
Suspended!

Boys on the nearest raft were kneeling, trying to reach out to George with their arms and swords.

It only took a moment for Will to take it all in. He tore off his coat and threw it down. And then he was in the water, his shoes being sucked into the mucky bottom as he tried to hurry. The shoes stayed in the mud. His feet came free. Will didn't take his gaze off the hurt boy.

As soon as the water was deep enough, he started swimming. Out of the corner of his eye he could see someone from the other raft was swimming toward George now, too.

They reached him at the same time. The other swimmer was Jeremy.

"Turn him over!" Jeremy panted. "Get his face out of the water."

But Will was already doing that. When George's face was facing toward the sky, Jeremy laid his fingers along the boy's neck.

Will looked at Jeremy, unable to voice the question that he knew was in his eyes. He remembered this nice kid being wrapped in a bear hug by his father when the soldier returned from Port Royal. His father had lived through a real battle. Had his son lost his life in a pretend one?

It seemed forever before Jeremy said through lips that were quickly turning blue, "He's alive."

Together they pulled George to shore. By the time they got him on land, Will was shaking like a leaf in a storm. The weather might be mild for January, but the water felt like recently melted ice.

He grabbed his dry coat and laid it over George. The youngster needed it more than he did.

Jeremy wasn't worrying about his own shivering, either, Will noticed. Instead he was ripping off his own wet shirt sleeve and tying it around George's head, trying to stop the blood rushing out of the wound.

They carried the boy back to the school between them. Some of the other boys ran ahead to tell Mr. Evans what had happened. Will sent others to fetch a doctor. As they hurried along in their wet clothes and stocking feet, Will prayed constantly under his breath.

A couple of the boys from the rafts ran alongside them, telling in excited, scared bursts what had happened. The rafts had bumped together. The boys had tried to keep their balance, bumping against each other and hanging onto each other as the rafts drifted apart again. And then George had fallen in while the others were still too unbalanced to help. They didn't realize right away that he'd been hurt. He must have bumped his head against one of the raft's logs, they said.

They repeated it all for Mr. Evans as Will and Jeremy and George warmed themselves in front of the schoolroom fireplace wrapped in dry blankets furnished by the storekeeper downstairs. George had finally awakened after the doctor arrived. The wound was properly bandaged now, though the doctor praised Jeremy for his shirt sleeve attempt.

Jeremy had looked embarrassed and pleased at the same time at the compliment. He'd glanced over at Will. Will smiled at him. It was almost like they were friends again, helping George together the way they had. A twinge of pain twisted in his chest. He missed Jeremy's friendship.

One side of Jeremy's mouth tilted up in the beginning of a smile, and then he looked away again.

Class started very late that afternoon. Someone went for George's parents. They came and took him home with them, with strict orders from the doctor not to let him sleep for awhile in case the wound was worse than he suspected.

Mr. Evans told Will and Jeremy they might sit before the fire during class until their clothes were completely dry. Both boys were warm enough to have discarded the blankets, but their clothes were still damp.

Will watched in horror as Mr. Evans picked up the book that he'd glued together earlier. In all the excitement, he'd forgotten his attempt to get back at Jeremy.

The schoolmaster announced the lesson and at the same time tried to open the book. He continued to tug at the cover while speaking. Then, as the boys prepared for the lesson, Mr. Evans frowned down at his book, studying it.

Will could tell just when the schoolmaster knew what was wrong by the shocked expression on his face and the way he set his lips in the hard, thin line that always showed he was upset.

I wish the floor would just open and swallow me up, Will thought. *Why, why had he chosen today to pull his prank?*

He watched the schoolmaster going about the room, asking about the culprit and looking for evidence of who was responsible for the wrongdoing. When he found the glue stick Will had used in Jeremy's book, the surprise on Jeremy's face was almost funny.

Jeremy shook his head vigorously. "I didn't do it, Mr. Evans! Honest I didn't!"

"Books are not to be purposely destroyed, Master Jeremy. This is the second time you've been careless of them. The first was during the battle your army held in this very room, when you treated the precious books of knowledge as cannonballs."

Jeremy flushed. Will knew how he felt trapped by his past. Even though Jeremy was innocent today, the past made him look guilty, and he was seeing all chance of convincing the schoolmaster otherwise disappear.

Shame wormed across Will's chest. "Revenge belongs to God. We are to forgive our enemies." His father's reminder seemed to ring in his ears, over and over.

I forgive Jeremy for what he's done to me, God. Forgive me for trying to pay him back, he prayed silently.

Mr. Evans sighed deeply and picked up his cane. "Hold out your hand, Master Jeremy."

Jeremy flinched and took a step back, doubling his hand up at his side. Watching him, Will felt a little sick inside. He'd thought it would feel good to watch Jeremy be punished. It didn't feel good at all.

"I didn't do it, sir." Jeremy's voice sounded stubborn.

124

"Hold out your hand."

Jeremy did so slowly, anger filling his large brown eyes, his lips set as tightly as Mr. Evans's had been set when he discovered the book had been glued.

The schoolmaster lifted his cane.

"No!" Will bolted forward, grabbing the cane with both hands.

Mr. Evans and Jeremy stared at him, both too shocked to say anything.

Will was face to face with Mr. Evans, both of them still holding onto the cane. "He didn't do it, sir," he blurted out. "I did."

"You!"

Will ignored Jeremy's cry and kept staring at the schoolmaster, embarrassed that he'd tried to get his former friend in trouble.

"I see." Mr. Evans calmly removed the cane from Will's grasp. He looked from one to the other. "We'll discuss this after school, along with the Mill Pond incident."

Even though class had started late that afternoon, Will thought five o'clock would never come. The sand in the hourglass had never run so slowly, he was sure. He couldn't concentrate on his lesson. He concentrated mostly on not looking at Jeremy.

Joshua was chosen to lead the prayer at the end of the school day. He thanked God for sparing George's life. When he'd finished praying, Mr. Evans said dryly, "I should think you would have asked God to forgive all of you for playing upon the water. Not one of your parents would allow such foolishness, I'm sure."

Joshua's face grew red. A number of the boys hung their heads and shuffled their feet.

"From now on," the schoolmaster continued, "none of you are to play about Mill Pond during the hours school is dismissed for the noon meal. I shall patrol the area personally during this time. In addition, I shall speak with the constable and ask him to see that boys are kept away from the pond."

Kept away from Mill Pond! Will bit back a cry of protest. It was one of the boys' favorite places in all Boston.

"You are dismissed," Evans said. "Except for Masters William and Jeremy."

The boys started to leave, guiltily silent. A number of them cast Will and Jeremy pitying looks. Will knew each of the boys felt they were as much to blame for what happened at the pond as Will and Jeremy and didn't care for the unfairness of the two boys being singled out for further scolding or punishment.

Only the many shoes moving across the floorboards and the crackle of the fire dying in the fireplace made any noise.

When the others had left, Mr. Evans turned to Will and Jeremy. He leaned on his cane with one hand, his other hand resting along the small of his back. *He looked tired,* Will thought in surprise. More than a little tired. He looked like he was worn out all the way through. Even more surprising, he didn't look angry.

"I don't know what has happened," he began, "that the two of you have become such troublemakers this year. The pranks you've pulled have been bad enough, but Mill Pond—" He shook his head, the curls of his wig sliding across his shoulders.

Will heard Jeremy clear his throat. Was Jeremy as uncomfortable as he was?

"I know that Mill Pond was not the result of another prank," Mr. Evans continued. "The fact remains that the other students look up to you—consider you their leaders. You should have known it wasn't safe for them to play on rafts. They would have listened if you had told them not to do it."

Will looked down at his dirt-caked stockings—his shoes were still at the bottom of Mill Pond—and swallowed hard.

"You are both to be commended for saving the boy's life. You acted quickly and bravely. For that reason, I wish I could allow the incident to pass without further comment or punishment. But the fact remains, the boy could have died. Other lives were endangered. That cannot be overlooked. Do you understand that?"

"Yes, sir."

"Yes, sir."

"I will be stopping at both your homes this evening to speak with your parents."

Will's head whipped up. He'd known his parents would have to hear what had happened at Mill Pond, but why was the schoolmaster coming to their homes?

Mr. Evans's chest heaved, lifting his black coat as he sighed his deep sigh one more time. "I shall recommend you both be suspended from school."

He continued speaking. Will could see his lips moving, but he couldn't hear anything he said. His ears roared. All he could think of was what his father's face would look like when he heard the awful news. His father would be ashamed of him.

He felt Mr. Evans's bony fingers on his shoulder and made himself listen to what he was saying. "I'm sorry, lads, that it's come to this. The most I can do for you at this point is to offer you the chance to speak to your parents before I come and tell them yourselves what has happened."

"Thank you, sir." Will's voice croaked the words.

He and Jeremy left together. They were out in the street before they said anything.

Jeremy cleared his throat. "About that glued book—"

Will looked at him, surprised. He'd forgotten about the book. It didn't even seem important now.

"Did you really glue it together, or did you just say so to stop old man Evans from striking me?"

"I did it. I wanted to get back at you for the pranks you had blamed on me."

Jeremy had the grace to flush at the reminder of his treatment of Will over the last few months. "I don't understand. Why didn't you let Evans punish me?"

"I guess after we saved the boy, I couldn't stay angry with you. I kept remembering what good friends we used to be."

"Well, I'm sorry I've been so rotten to you."

Will nodded and started walking. It made him uncomfortable to have Jeremy apologize to him.

"Will! Will!"

He spun around at Beth's voice. She was dashing along the narrow, crooked street, holding up her long skirt so she could run faster. Her ribbons and blond curls streamed behind her.

She grabbed his arm when she reached him. "It's Mary," she panted. "She's having the baby!"

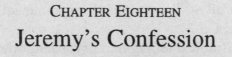

CHAPTER EIGHTEEN
Jeremy's Confession

Four hours later, Will sat by the hearth in the parlor, his foot rocking the cradle. He stared down at the baby bound in a soft blanket. The funny, pink, wrinkled face didn't look a bit like Mary or Rob.

Mary had named the little boy after his father. Little Robert had already been born when Will arrived home with Beth that afternoon. In the few hours since, everyone in the family had good-naturedly fought over who should hold him next, who had held him the longest, and whether they shouldn't put him in the cradle and let him sleep.

Will almost hadn't had the courage to break in on his family's happy evening with the news about school. He had hated telling his father about Mill Pond and hated more telling him he'd purposely glued the schoolmaster's book together to get back at Jeremy. He'd stumbled over the words when he told Father that Mr. Evans was suspending him.

But most of all, he'd hated the disappointment he'd seen in his father's eyes.

He'd barely finished telling him everything when Mr. Evans arrived. In fact, the old man arrived so soon after Will's confession that Mr. Smith hadn't had a chance to comment on the events or Will's suspension.

And then the most surprising thing of the day happened.

Mr. Evans didn't look a bit grim or tired when he arrived. His skinny, wrinkled face was one big smile.

Will thought grumpily that the old man needn't look so happy about suspending him. He followed his father and Mr. Evans into the parlor, grateful his father arranged for the three of them to speak alone. Things were bad enough without Beth's big ears, big eyes, and big mouth around. He didn't want her teasing him or blabbing to her friends about him.

Mr. Evans sat by the fireplace in their best chair, his hands on the cane between his legs, and beamed.

"My son has told me about the prank today and the Mill Pond incident," Mr. Smith started in his usual quiet, unruffled way. "I hope the boy who was injured is doing well?"

"Hmmm? Oh, yes, yes," the schoolmaster said. "I stopped by his house on my way here. Doing fine, he is."

"I was sorry to hear you feel it necessary to suspend my son."

"Yes, well. . ." Mr. Evans beamed at Will again. Will couldn't figure out what was going on. He'd never seen the schoolmaster like this. "Things have changed since I last spoke to your son."

"Changed?" Mr. Smith asked, his eyebrows lifting.

"Changed?" Will echoed.

Mr. Evans nodded, his head going up and down like a gull on a wave, Will thought. "Yes. I went to Jeremy Clark's home before coming here. He tells me that until today, all the pranks for which I blamed William were Jeremy's doing."

Will clutched the seat of his armless wooden chair until his fingers hurt. Jeremy had told the truth! He could hardly believe it.

"Yes, yes," Mr. Evans's head was still bobbing, and the funny smile was still in place. "I don't know why he was so angry with William, but whatever the reason, he managed to entangle William in a multitude of pranks."

Mr. Smith smiled at Will. "I've always believed my son was innocent of those pranks. I'm glad Jeremy decided to finally tell the truth."

Will tried to act mature and not smile as wide as his mouth wanted to smile. He couldn't remember when he'd ever felt so good.

"In light of Jeremy's news," Mr. Evans continued, "I've decided to lift Will's suspension. After all, he's already been punished for all those pranks he didn't commit."

Will's mouth dropped open. He snapped it shut. "Thank you, sir."

Mr. Smith thanked him, too, with a smile almost as big as Mr. Evans's.

"I was glad to find my best student hadn't become a rebel." The schoolmaster sobered, but only a little. *He looks like he's trying to be stern, but can't quite make himself,* Will thought. "Of course, there's the matter of Mill Pond. We mustn't forget the poor boy who almost drowned."

"No, sir."

"So instead of being suspended indefinitely, I suggest a shortened suspension. Shall we say, the rest of the week?"

Only three days. Will looked at his father. What would he say?

Mr. Smith stood and extended his hand to Mr. Evans. "That sounds more than reasonable, sir."

Thank you, Lord! Will prayed silently, standing. "Thank you, sir."

"Well, you've been a fine student until the last few months, Master Smith. I shall miss you when you leave North Writing School for good."

Will flushed, but the men were no longer looking at him, he saw gratefully.

"I've a brand new grandson, Mr. Evans. Won't you let me introduce you?"

When the schoolmaster had seen the baby and offered the proper polite compliments, he took his leave.

Half-an-hour later, there was another knock at the front door. This time it was Jeremy. Will slipped outside where they could talk in spite of the chilly January air.

"Was Evans here yet?" This from Jeremy.

"Yes. I. . .that is. . .thanks for telling him. . .you know."

"You did the same for me this afternoon. Did he say anything about the suspension?"

Will wished he knew what Mr. Evans had decided about Jeremy. He was almost embarrassed to tell him his good news. "He, uh, shortened it, since I'd already been punished a few times."

"I'm glad."

The silence grew a bit long. "What about you, Jeremy?"

"My suspension? It's for good, I'm afraid. Father says I go to

132

work in his cooper's shop tomorrow morning. No more school for me."

Will wanted to tell him he was sorry, but he knew Jeremy wouldn't want his pity, anymore than he'd have wanted Jeremy's if the situation were reversed. "Well, you were almost through at North Writing School anyway. Just a few months left."

"Yes."

"It won't be the same without you there." It was the closest Will could come to saying he was sorry.

"You'll stop by the shop after school some, won't you, Will?"

"Sure. Course, I've only a few months left of school myself." Will kicked his toe idly against the front stoop. "Uh, why were you so mad at me, Jeremy?"

He didn't answer for a minute. Will began to think he wasn't going to answer at all. He wouldn't have dared ask the question if they weren't standing out in the dark, where they couldn't see each other's faces clearly.

Jeremy's voice was so quiet when he finally spoke that Will could barely hear him. "I, uh, was upset that you heard your father say he wouldn't take me on as an apprentice. I always wanted to be a cabinetmaker and work with your father. And then you met General Nicholson and went aboard the man-of-war, and—well, I got jealous and then angry, and it just grew, I guess."

Will could understand that. He might have felt the same way if he'd been in Jeremy's shoes. Maybe he was somewhat to blame for the way Jeremy had acted. "I guess I showed off a bit about knowing the general and such," he admitted.

"Naw. Well, not much."

"So, did you ask to be apprenticed to any other cabinet-makers?"

"No. At first, I didn't ask because I only wanted to work with your father. Then later, I guess I just didn't want to risk having any other cabinetmakers turn me down."

"Um, do you want to be a cooper?"

"No." Jeremy's answer was swift and strong.

"Maybe you should talk to some other cabinetmakers."

Jeremy didn't answer.

Will shivered in the cold. If he was cold, Jeremy must be, too. "Let's go inside. I don't know about you, but I never again want to be as cold as I was in Mill Pond this afternoon."

Jeremy laughed and followed him inside. "Me, either. But I should be getting home. Father only allowed me to come because I won't see you at school for a few days, and he wanted me to say something to you about, well, you know. . ."

"Why don't you come in and see the baby before you go?"

Jeremy agreed.

Will stopped in the entryway. Flames from the parlor fireplace spread a little light to the hall. "You were great at the pond today," he said quietly. "That was good thinking, using your shirt sleeve to tie up his wound."

Jeremy's face turned red beneath his freckles. "You were pretty good out there yourself."

Will wondered what Jeremy's father had said about Jeremy's part in rescuing the boy. Had it softened his father's anger at Jeremy's suspension? He hoped so.

Only Will's father and the baby were in the parlor. His mother was in the kitchen, and Beth had been sent to bed. "Watch the baby, Will. I need to speak to your mother," Father said and left Jeremy and Will alone.

Jeremy dutifully walked over to the cradle and looked at the baby. "Looks wrinkled."

Will laughed.

"Is it a girl or a boy?"

"A boy. Mary named him Robert, after his father."

Jeremy nodded. He ran his hand over the bonnet of the cradle. "Did Rob make this?"

"Yes." Will's throat felt suddenly tight.

"He was a good cabinetmaker, wasn't he?"

"Yes. Father misses him at the shop." Will darted a glance at Jeremy. "I suppose a lot of shop owners are short of men these days, what with so many journeymen in the military."

Jeremy shrugged. "I suppose."

Will turned and poked at the logs in the fireplace with the poker. He said as casually as he could manage, "I could ask my father if he knows of any cabinetmakers looking for a good apprentice. Maybe ask him who he thinks are the best in Boston—besides himself, that is."

Jeremy glanced at him and ran the tip of his tongue along his lips. "You think?"

"Sure."

Jeremy stuck his hands in his coat pockets. "Well, I'd better be getting home."

The church bells were ringing when Will closed the door behind Jeremy. Nine o'clock. Curfew hour. Jeremy would have to make it home quickly and watch out for the men who patrolled the streets from nine at night to five in the morning.

He went back to the hearth, sat down, and looked at little Robert. The babe was yawning, his tiny mouth open in an egg-shaped O, his wrinkled face wrinkling even more. He squirmed about in his blankets.

Will reached out a finger and rubbed the few black hairs on Robert's almost bald head. A sharp pain twisted his stomach. "I wish your father could have seen you at least once."

Poor little Robert, growing up without a father. Like Beth's friend Martha and her brother Samuel. Will couldn't imagine it.

"Don't worry, baby Robert," he whispered. "I can't give you back your father, but you'll always be taken care of. Your father knew that, or he wouldn't have gone to war."

He had known it, Will realized. Rob's family had all been killed, and he'd had only the Smiths, so he had to have known what it was like to be without a father. God never leaves us or forsakes us, Rob had reminded him once. God had given him Mr. Smith to look out for him when his own parents were killed. Rob had known when he left for battle that Mary and the family would take care of little Robert if anything happened to him.

"You ever need anything, little Robert," Will whispered to his nephew, "you come to me. I'll see you get everything you need to grow into the man your father would have wanted. I'll help you learn to read and write, so you can read the Bible and the laws. And I'll be sure you learn a trade so you can support yourself and your family when you're a man."

He thought of Jeremy and his longing to be a cabinetmaker. "Think you might want to be a cabinetmaker like your father?" Will laughed at his own foolishness, asking a baby only a few hours old what he wanted to be as a man.

Maybe by the time Robert was old enough to fight for England and the Massachusetts Bay Colony, they'd live at peace with the French and Indians. Maybe the countries would learn to forgive each other, like he and Jeremy had.

The baby fussed, wiggling a bit in his blankets and screwing up his funny little face. Will lifted him a bit awkwardly to his lap. The boy blinked his tiny dark lashes.

"Maybe your father's prayer will be answered, little Robert, and you'll never have to be a soldier and go to war like him."

Rob had given his life so his son could live in a land of peace. Will lifted a silent prayer that it would be so.

Good News for Readers

There's more!

The American Adventure continues in *Danger in the Harbor*. Queen Anne's War is over, but many people in Boston are going hungry. Some grain merchants are more interested in making money than in helping their neighbors. People get so angry that they damage the merchants' ships in the middle of the night—and Beth and Will are there when it happens!

Then they learn that riots are planned. What should Beth and Will do? And when Father tries to stop the angry mob, will he be killed?